204729

CASTOR OIL AND LAVENDER

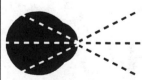

This Large Print Book carries the
Seal of Approval of N.A.V.H.

OHIO BOOK 4

CASTOR OIL AND LAVENDER

THE YOUNG BUCKEYE STATE BLOSSOMS WITH LOVE AND ADVENTURE IN THIS COMPLETE NOVEL

DIANNE CHRISTNER

THORNDIKE PRESS

An imprint of Thomson Gale, a part of The Thomson Corporation

THOMSON

GALE

Detroit • New York • San Francisco • New Haven, Conn. • Waterville, Maine • London

THOMSON
GALE

LIBRARY OF CONGRESS CATALOGING-IN-PUBLICATION DATA

Christner, Dianne L., 1951–
    Castor oil and lavender : the young Buckeye State blossoms with love and adventure in this complete novel / by Dianne Christner.
        p. cm. — (Ohio ; #4) (Thorndike Press large print Christian historical fiction)
    ISBN-13: 978-0-7862-9783-2 (hardcover : alk. paper)
    ISBN-10: 0-7862-9783-2 (hardcover : alk. paper)
    1. Ohio — Fiction. 2. Sisters — Fiction. 3. Large type books. I. Title.
PS3603.H76C37 2007
813'.6—dc22   2007026774

Published in 2007 by arrangement with Barbour Publishing, Inc.

Printed in the United States of America on permanent paper
10 9 8 7 6 5 4 3 2 1

As always, I appreciate my family's encouragement and would also like to thank Rebecca Germany for the opportunities she's given me, and for her expertise as a writer and editor.

CHAPTER 1

Randolph Cline peered at him from across the massive polished desk. No matter how intimidating it was to be the recipient of that condescending gaze, the doctor was determined not to show it. Dr. David Wheeler gripped the chair's smooth walnut armrests and leaned forward. "With every hour that passes, the condition of our city only worsens."

"Let me get this straight. You're suggesting that I hire immigrants to sweep Cincinnati's streets?" Cline's balding forehead wrinkled. "And would you also like me to finance the counting of stars? Perhaps for the sake of science?" Apparently he didn't expect an answer to his question, for after shifting in his chair — which seemed to be a habitual gesture — he continued with his argument. "I'll agree that our city is swarming with the ragged and pitiful, but until you can show me how I will profit in this venture, I cannot help you."

David realized that 1837 was a year of hard times for the nation as a whole, but he also knew that men like Cline continued to prosper. All in all, Cincinnati still boomed. The doctor pressed his boots against the other man's imported rug and pasted on a smile. "Oh, but you will greatly profit. You might spare your own life or the lives of your family." Cline's eyes looked heavenward indicating disbelief, but David continued. "It is only a matter of time until another bout of cholera hits Cincinnati. With your donation, other respectable citizens will follow suit and also contribute. What seems to you an impossible task can be accomplished, and everyone benefits."

Randolph Cline pushed back his chair and eased himself onto his feet. David saw a flicker of pain wash across the man's face and mentally clicked off a list of maladies that might be tormenting him: *Back pain? Too early in the day for indigestion. Possibly hemorrhoids?*

"Beautify the city. Sounds nice. But not practical," Cline said. David stiffened when Cline touched his shoulder. "Now, I need to prepare for my day and upcoming appointments."

He followed Cline to the door, voicing a

final plea. "The city's board of health supports this project. Dr. Drake says —"

Cline's hands flew up as if to ward off some odious pest. "Do not bring up that man's name. Had I known he was behind this, I wouldn't have given you the hour." He pointed a finger at David. "You are young and impressionable so let me give you a word of counsel. Treat the sick, and let the lawyers take care of the city's problems."

The doctor squared his shoulders beneath his brown frock coat and said more curtly than intended, "A physician not only treats the sick but hopes to prevent disease. I thank you for your time."

He left the land developer-textile manufacturer's office more determined than ever to promote his project of cleaning up Cincinnati's filthy streets. Lives depended upon it. But one thing was certain. He could cross Randolph Cline off his list of prospective donators. David smiled grimly. He would not mention Dr. Drake's name to his next candidate. Which was . . . He pulled a list from his pocket. Number two, Vernon Thorpe. Number three, Zachary Caulfield.

David set his back to September's early morning sun. It peeked over the buildings of the finer district of Cincinnati. Mentally he rehashed the meeting as he strode toward his one-room dwelling, which was attached to the clinic where he received patients.

Later, entering the building by a side door, a fluffy, brown-streaked cat pressed against his leg. "Hello, Gratuity." The cat waltzed in and out of his steps. "Did you find yourself a meal last night?" David stooped to scratch the purring cat's head, then straightened. He placed his fine, brown frock coat on a hook, jerked off his cravat, and crossed the room to an inadequate bed. A maple wardrobe was wedged between the wall and bed, its doors too warped to close.

He sat, and the cat joined him on the bed. "It didn't go well, Gratuity. Mr. Cline would not be persuaded. Narrow-minded. Cannot see the necessity of prevention. Only interested in his fat purse." David pulled off his tall leather boots and wiggled out of his tight pantaloons, exchanging them for a comfortable pair of loose trousers from the wardrobe — some he had bartered from a beggar at the Ohio River docks. His elbow poked through a hole as he slipped into the sleeve of an old coat. "Drake says it only takes a couple enthusiastic persons and then everything else will fall into place." Gratuity finished a spit bath and curled up into a purring ball of fluff. "Some sympathy I get

10

from you. Have a good nap."

After retrieving his black physician's bag from his clinic, David started north toward the canal. His thoughts shifted to an entirely different problem — the patient he was going to visit. If only people didn't bring all their superstitions with them when they emigrated from the old country. He was positive that Mrs. Schroeder's illness was all in her head, a so-called curse resulting from a dispute with a neighbor.

Raised by missionary parents in West Africa, David knew how destructive such pagan beliefs could be. Mrs. Schroeder's physical decline had become more evident with each of his house calls. Death's door would open wide unless he could think of a cure. Reasoning with this patient was futile.

His path followed the narrow stone canal. The new day burst into wildlife song, inspiring him. He quickened his step, chuckling at the simplicity of the remedy, veered off the cobblestone pathway, and sloshed through the weedy grasses where he toed the soggy leaves and twigs until he spotted his prize. "Aha! There you are." Dropping into a squat, he let go of his black bag and snatched up his unsuspecting prey. It croaked and lunged. Grasping the slimy, long-legged creature more tightly, he held

11

the frog up to his face. Its legs dangled.

All in an instant, memories of long-gone boyhood days by the Niger River of Africa lightened his morning's cares. David stared into the bulging eyes. "You, little fellow, are going to do an errand of mercy for me."

A rumble of male laughter and several feminine giggles brought David's gaze back toward the footpath. He stuffed the amphibian into his pocket, but upon feeling a gaping hole, shifted it instead to the opposite side.

Sure. It was unconventional. But if he could keep the woman's physical body from perishing, there was still hope for her soul. Retrieving his bag, he whistled his way back to the path and, stride quickening again, headed past the tallow factory and pork-packing plant toward the canal crossing at the locks.

On Thirteenth Street, counting buildings to distinguish Mrs. Schroeder's place of dwelling from the similar ones within the rows of three- to five-story brick buildings, he veered to enter a dismal establishment's door, then climbed the steps two at a time until he reached the landing of the third floor. After a quick rap, he stuck his head inside the apartment.

"Mrs. Schroeder? It's me, Dr. Wheeler. I

came to see how you were doing today."

A moan sounded from a round lump of covers on a narrow cot in the far corner of the room. David easily interpreted the German mumbling. "That frog in my stomach is eating my insides. Will you find my son and tell him that I love him?"

"I'm sure you can tell him yourself," he replied using the woman's native language.

"No. I'm dying."

"Nonsense. I brought you a cure."

A tousled head shot up from the disheveled lump. The eyes were hopeful, but the head shook in disbelief.

"A strong potion."

She sat up. "A potion? Well, maybe. *Ja,* I have heard of such things."

"Let's not waste any more time then." David began a merry version of a German song as he took a spoon and bottle from his bag and helped the woman swallow a dose of ipecac.

Sometimes Josephine Cline wished she could be more like her father, but she hopelessly took after her mother. Father said that viewing life through her heart instead of her eyes was a handicap. Today was a perfect example. Her tender gaze took in the twelve-year-old lad's haunted expression, and her compassion squelched any misgivings she had been harboring about inconveniences.

"Say, Charles, won't your mama be surprised to get a visit from you? It might be just the thing to nurse her back to health."

"Happy I am to work for your papa. But for Mama, I worry. *Ja,* to see her is *gut.* Maybe for Mama is *gut,* too."

Hugging her velvet cloak against her body to keep out the September morning's chill, Josephine noticed the threadbare condition of Charles's wool coat, mentally making a note to bring it to her mother's attention. Of all the Elm Street orphans her mama clothed, she would be embarrassed to discover that someone under her care was ill clad. "Are you warm enough?"

The lad's hand swiped the air. *"Ja."* His head bent low as if it was his duty to watch his boots navigate the granite footpath.

Josephine's heart tugged. Her father's apprentice might possess a youthful, even angelic face, but most of the time he exhibited manlike courage. Father thought highly of Charles to allow the apprentice time off his job at the textile factory to check up on his sick mother. But Father always possessed insight and practicality. That was why he had added the stipulation that Josephine must accompany the boy. Father wanted to

14

make sure Charles didn't take flight or squander a precious day's time. She was along to chaperone. It would make a good report to the charity society to which she belonged. *Oh, Lord.* She glanced heavenward and sighed. *Forgive my petty thoughts.*

Charles's gait quickened. Josephine swept her hood away from her face and glanced sideways at the boy. His expression was happily animated, and his feet seemed to remember their way home now. They passed the tallow factory and pork-packing plant, fast approaching the canal locks.

On Thirteenth Street, Josephine exhaled visible puffs of air and lifted her full skirt and three petticoats to scurry up the steps, keeping at Charles's heels all the while wondering how he could tell his tenement from all the others. Was it perhaps more run-down? Even so, the lad seemed glad to be home. But the instant they crept into the stale room, she sensed that they were not alone. A quick glance took in the scene. A physician bent over a woman, one who suddenly rose up from her bed and heaved on top of the doctor's boots. Josephine instinctively clutched Charles by the shoulders to keep him from rushing forward as the woman retched.

Gradually Josephine became aware that

the man in the room did not have the appearance of a doctor though he carried a black medical bag. His shabby attire resembled that of a beggar's. And he certainly did not behave like a doctor, singing at the woman's bedside.

Josephine watched him thrust his hand into a pocket and withdraw a . . . a *frog!* With a jubilant glint in his blue eyes, he tossed the amphibian into the mess on his boots, then from the tone of his voice — for she could not understand the foreign conversation — he must have ordered the poor woman to rise up off her sickbed. And more to the wonder of it all, she did. Then while Charles watched with his mouth agape, arm in arm his mother and the long-legged man danced a jig as if this was some grand celebration.

Before she could fully fathom the meaning of all that had just transpired, Charles broke loose from her grip and rushed into the mess. Josephine grimaced.

"Mama!" The boy released a stream of German.

The man turned and stared at Josephine as if he had just noticed them. Her face heated.

"Miss Josephine! Mama's healed! The curse is over." Josephine shuddered, wishing for an instant that she had stayed at home in her warm cozy bed and that Charles had not returned to his old home at all but stayed where he was safe and life was normal.

The blond man rolled up his threadbare sleeves and headed for the washbasin. Josephine felt like she ought to be doing something to help restore order. But before she could move, the mother rushed across the room cackling some foreign protest. It appeared that she felt well enough now to see to her own needs.

Josephine blinked twice. The medical imposter accepted payment for the fraudulent cure without hesitation over the fact that the woman might not be able to afford her next meal. He rattled off more German and headed toward the door seeming very pleased with himself.

Josephine's anger surfaced over the injustice. "Charles. Talk to your mama while I see the doctor out."

The man flinched. One of his blond eyebrows slanted upward as he studied her.

If he expects to get away with this atrocity, then he is wrong, she fumed. *I will show him that he cannot take advantage of poor immigrants.* "I would have a word with you," she said, her tone barbed.

He wore a mustache, and his blond side-burns extended into a thin beard, which framed his face. He gave her an odd half smile, bid Mrs. Schroeder and Charles a warm farewell, and strode out the door without the courtesy of a reply.

Josephine's many skirts swept up a cloud of dust from the floorboards, and she fled down the stairs after him, her hot gaze never leaving his back. "Will you wait? I wish to speak with you!"

At the bottom of the landing, he shouldered open the door, stepped outside, and wheeled about abruptly. She stopped just inches from colliding into him. Retreating a few steps, she glared up into his twinkling blue eyes. "You, Sir, are a fraud!"

He cocked one blond eyebrow at her for the second time that morning and looked down his fine Roman nose. Then he had the gall to smile. His voice was soft, his English perfect, and he addressed her as if she were a small child. "Miss. The eye can be deceiving. I assure you that you are working yourself up over nothing. Let me explain
—"

"I saw what you did with that frog. You acted like she was under some curse. And you took payment. Only a worm would grovel so low."

His eyes narrowed. He mumbled. Josephine heard the words "insulting mouth." Who was he to reprimand her?

"I plan to turn you in to the proper authorities."

"An unbridled mouth is an unattractive trait in a woman." He bit off his sentence as if he would have said more but thought better of it and turned away.

"You have not heard the end of this!"

This time he did not even flinch.

Josephine placed her hands upon her hips. *Arrogant pauper.* Her face burned with humiliation over the way he had treated her, walking away from her as if she and everything she had said were insignificant. *Doctor. Hah!* She would see that he was tracked down and brought to justice for his misdeed. How could anyone behave in such a manner? Surely her father would know what to do with a man like this.

The tenement door flew open. Charles stuck his head out. "Mama wishes to meet you."

Josephine unclamped her so-called *insulting, unbridled* mouth and exhaled deeply, trying to appear congenial for the lad's sake. "Of course, Charles. I want to meet her, too."

CHAPTER 2

His good nature prevailing, before David even crossed the canal, he chuckled to himself over the incident he had just incurred. The woman's anger had progressed to a boil much like the steam engine that powered Cincinnati's new steamship, the *Moselle* — the ship that was on everyone's lips and appeared in so many headlines. He could have sworn he saw steam puffing from her ears. Perhaps God should have designed female creatures with safety valves. He chuckled.

The funny thing was, he couldn't blame her for thinking he was a fraud. At first her accusation had galled him because he detested the quacks that had infiltrated Cincinnati, giving people false hope. In fact, his mentor, Dr. Drake, frequently discussed that very thing with him — how to protect citizens from those who practiced medicine without the proper qualifications. Anyway, how was that lovely creature to know that David had a framed medical diploma hanging above the bookcase in his clinic?

It was kind of cute the way she stood up to him, defending Mrs. Schroeder. He should have made her listen to his explanation instead of spouting off at her. What had he said anyway? Something about an unbridled tongue? That had certainly brought color to her cheeks. He chuckled again. No woman liked that kind of talk. Perhaps he was to blame for shoveling coal onto her smoldering fire. But then what did he know about women or what they liked? Not much. Anyway, no doubt he would never see this one again.

"Good morning, Dr. Wheeler."

"Good morning to you." David nodded at the boy vendor and exchanged a coin for a paper, which he thrust beneath his arm. No patients waited on the clinic's stoop. This meant he might squeeze in breakfast before he went to work.

Early mornings were his favorite. He took pleasure in donning old clothes and going on the prowl for patients — the kind that would not feel comfortable or be able to afford coming to the clinic. The needs were great among the people who inhabited areas like the slummy district along the Ohio

River docks or along the canal. Very seldom was a morning unproductive.

Though some of his medical comrades thought he was eccentric, David found his method of treatment most practical. It was similar to the way his parents had performed their services in Africa.

Gratuity greeted him with purrs, rubbing against his legs. In keeping with his daily ritual, David read snatches of news to the cat while cracking eggs into an iron skillet. As the eggs sizzled, he hurried to change into a third set of clothing: this time a linen shirt and trousers. He fastened his suspenders and slipped into a wool waistcoat. He hated cravats and never wore them to the clinic.

Scorched egg stench reached his nostrils, and he hurried back to his breakfast, scraping the unappetizing meal onto a plate. As he forked down his fare, he finished flipping through the pages of the *Cincinnati Gazette*.

"Listen to this, Gratuity. Benefit dinner for the women's workhouse to be held at the home of Zachary Caulfield." *Number three on my list,* he told himself as he slid his plate to the floor and mumbled, "Come get your leftovers." The cat's hesitancy made him sorry he had burned their breakfast once again. He stacked the dishes and pulled on his brown leather boots. "Perhaps I need to attend that dinner next week, Gratuity. Might meet some folks with money to spare for our cause." He grabbed his bag. "Let's go see what this day has to offer. Shall we?" The cat slipped out the open door and disappeared. David strode toward the clinic and withdrew a key from his pocket.

Josephine slipped off her cloak and draped it over her arm. "What an exhausting morning."

Her mother looked up from stitching a comforter. "Sit down, Dear. Tell me about it. How is Mrs. Schroeder?"

Sinking into a mahogany and rose upholstered chair, Josie propped up her legs and crossed her feet on a matching stool, reveling in the comfort. "Mrs. Schroeder is fully recovered."

"But I thought she was on her deathbed. Was it just a rumor?"

"I do not know, Mother. She does not speak English, you know. But she is fine now. Some beggar masquerading as a doctor spoke mumbo jumbo over her, and she seemed good as new."

"You look tired. Was it far?"

"No. But I did help her clean up the place.

She has so little." Josephine's gaze settled on the silver wall sconces, and she wished there was more she could have done to help the sweet woman.

Mrs. Cline went back to her stitching with renewed fervor.

"But I think what wore me out was that infuriating doctor. I mean to tell Father about him."

"Yes." Her mother nodded sympathetically. "I'm sure your father will know what to do." She glanced up. "Josie, you look like you could use a nap."

"No time. This afternoon I'm helping the cook."

"I'll never know where you get that love for cooking."

"Or you, your love for sewing."

Mrs. Cline's face lit with pleasure. "Perhaps we should make one of these for Mrs. Schroeder, too. What do you think?"

"Oh, Mother. I believe anything would be appreciated. And winter is just around the corner. That reminds me. Charles needs a new coat."

"Charles?"

"Father's German apprentice."

"Oh, yes. Of course. I will take care of it."

Josephine spent the rest of the day helping the cook with dinner. That evening she gave

24

her hair a final inspection and hurried back downstairs. When she entered the dining room, a servant pulled out her chair.

"Hello, Father."

"Josie." He nodded at the servant, who disappeared into the kitchen and returned with steaming dishes of spiced pork and roasted vegetables. Heads bowed, silent prayers were issued. "Your mother tells me that you had quite a morning."

"I lost my temper." Details of her morning spilled out as Josie shared dinner with her parents. She brushed aside their cooking compliments and concluded her narrative with, "I want to turn him in to the authorities. How do I proceed?"

Mrs. Cline interjected, "I told her you would know what to do."

"Did you get the man's name?"

"I had to get the information from Charles. It's Spokes."

"Hmm. Never heard of him."

"The way he was dressed, I'm sure he doesn't have a real practice."

"If he doesn't have a practice, then there's not much we can do to hinder him except run him out of town."

"Don't you have a man who could do an investigation?"

"Yes, but that all costs money. Is this really

25

that important to you?"

Josie felt her cheeks heat, and she nodded. "Yes."

"I'll see what I can do. Say, I know what will get your mind off the scoundrel. We're invited to a formal dinner."

"Something we'll need new gowns for?" Mrs. Cline's eyes sparkled.

Josie grinned. "Do tell us about it, Father."

A steady stream of carriages deposited Cincinnati's posh and prosperous at the entrance of Zachary Caulfield's luxurious Victorian estate. David had walked. He waited in the dark shadows of a tall tree to take it all in. A row of gas lamps lined the street where stylish figures paraded by. Cincinnati was a crossroads between the backwoods and the civilized, but its prominent society did not lack in manners or elegance.

He adjusted his despised cravat before stepping out from the shadows. A doorman checked his invitation. He wished Dr. Drake had been able to accompany him, but the doctor was traveling again. It had taken some finagling, but David had been able to obtain an invitation through connections with Clay Buchanan, a friend of Drake's who was on the board of health.

Stepping into the room where about twenty-five people had gathered, David studied his surroundings: elegant tables clad with white cloths, enough appetizers to make his stomach rumble, and people clustered off not only according to occupation and social fabric, but also according to Yankees and Southerners.

With the food as a lodestar, he worked his way through the crowd, happy to stumble so quickly upon Clay Buchanan.

"Come here, Doctor. We were just discussing the East versus the West."

Handshakes admitted him into a small circle of men. Clay Buchanan proceeded to press his point. "The East is static, conservative, old; the West is dynamic, progressive, young."

It went without saying, and David only half listened to the flames of conversation that leapt up about him. He was more interested in the information his eyes could glean. When he spotted two gentlemen whose names were on his list, his heartbeat quickened. *Vernon Thorpe and Quinton Wallace.* His mind warmed to the possibilities of how he might introduce his subject.

As he watched them, the two men turned their gazes to a small cluster of women. Wondering what had captured their attention, David fixed his gaze in that direction. To his great surprise, he recognized one of the women as the boiling steam engine from Mrs. Schroeder's. Only tonight she looked like an angel.

In a swirl of blue silk with a string of pearls at her creamy neck, she glided through the maze of guests. Fascinated, he crooked his neck and leaned sideways to keep her in his view. Her hair was swept up in a most becoming arrangement of brown curls. He could see why she had turned the other gentlemen's heads.

David turned to Clay Buchanan. "Say. Do you know who that young woman is by the fireplace?"

"The pretty one in blue?"

"Yes, she's the one."

"That's Josephine Cline, Randolph's daughter."

No other name could have doused his fire so quickly and thoroughly. He frowned, assessing what he knew about the father and transferring the man's attributes to the daughter.

She looked up. Their gazes locked. He struggled to pull his away but couldn't. She stared back at him in such a brash manner that he cocked his brow at her, shifting the blame of his impropriety upon her.

Instantly, her eyes widened with recognition. The color of her cheeks deepened, and her brown eyes narrowed again. In a queenly manner, she thrust her chin in the air, grabbed a fistful of skirt and lacy petticoat, and marched toward him — a flurry of blue silk.

With each of her steps, it grew more evident she had not forgiven him and meant to continue where they had last left off. David frantically searched the room for a means of escape. *The terrace.* He wheeled about and started toward it.

"Mr. Spokes. Is that you?"

Who was Mr. Spokes? Curiosity proved to be his downfall. He chanced a backward glance.

She rushed forward. "Wait!"

His spirits sagged. It *was* him she was after. And she *was* going to make a scene.

CHAPTER 3

David took several steps toward the terrace, hoping he and Miss Cline could take their conversation to a private location.

"It is you." Miss Cline brushed past him and blocked his path.

"Excuse me? Are you speaking to me?" *Maybe if I feign ignorance she will go away.*

"You know very well that I am."

David sighed. "What may I do for you, Miss? I do not believe we have been introduced." *That should put her in her place.*

"Oh, but we have. At Mrs. Schroeder's."

"Ah, yes. I remember."

He felt embarrassed under her scrutiny.

"I almost didn't recognize you." A gleam of cunning suddenly appeared in her eyes, one that David did not trust. "I'm Josephine Cline. Come. I'd like to introduce you to my father."

"Ah, Miss Cline. I've already met your father."

She looked quizzically at him. "Well, then you must say hello. I'm sure he would be interested to hear about Mrs. Schroeder's health. Do come along." She tucked her gloved hand beneath his arm and tugged.

David could not believe her forwardness. "Look, Miss Cline. I would like to explain about that day." He grew impatient. "Can we please stop a moment?"

"I didn't take you for a shy man," she argued, while still guiding him across the room. She gave a little wave. He felt her grip tighten upon his arm "There. Father saw us. He's coming. You two can have a lovely chat about Mrs. Schroeder."

David jerked loose from her grip and straightened his frock coat. His voice resembled a low growl. "Your little game has been most amusing. Now if you will excuse me, I was about to get a bit of fresh air out on the terrace."

"Josephine? Did you want me?"

Mr. Cline loomed into David's vision before he could flee. Randolph Cline's gaze bore questioningly into David's, making his skin crawl worse than it had that day in the man's plush office.

"Yes, Father. I wanted you to meet Mr. Spokes. Remember? I mentioned him?"

David shrugged and shook Mr. Cline's

hand. "So nice to see you again."

"Dr. Wheeler." Randolph Cline's expression gradually changed to one of amusement. "Spokes. That's a good one, Josie. No wonder I didn't know whom you were talking about."

Miss Cline's cheeks turned bright red. "Our mystery has been solved, Father. You can call off your investigators." David noticed her painstaking enunciation of the word "investigators" and felt uncomfortably warm beneath her gloating defiant gaze.

The two gentlemen David had earlier noticed and wished to speak to regarding the funding of his city cleanup plan broke away from a group of affluent men and began to approach. Josie gestured. "Please join us. Have you met Dr. Spo — Wheeler?" Her cheeks momentarily reddened again.

For one foolish moment, David hoped fate was turning in his favor. He strode forward and thrust out his hand in greeting. But warnings flashed through his mind. Randolph Cline would react negatively if he introduced the subject of his project to clean up the city. Meanwhile, Cline's daughter continued her irritating game.

"Gentlemen, Dr. Wheeler has a new cure. Would you like to hear about it?"

"A new cure? Do tell us."

"Come now, Doctor. Don't be shy," she coaxed. "Tell them about the frog you keep in your pocket."

David managed a smile. "She's teasing you. It's a private joke between us."

"Modesty does not become you, Doctor. Tell the gentlemen how you tricked Mrs. Schroeder, convincing her she was cursed. It was quite disgusting, the way he abused the poor immigrant woman."

All three men frowned at the change of tone in Josephine's voice.

"Miss Cline, I do apologize for not explaining earlier. You see, I grew up in Africa where things like this were common."

Several eyebrows slanted. Randolph Cline's resembled a flock of flying geese. "You're talking about curses?"

"Why, yes." Josephine nodded.

"You put a curse on a woman?" one of the other men asked.

"No! I did not. I assure you that . . ." David felt the noose around his neck tighten. He fiddled with his cravat.

"Yes! He did. I saw it with my own eyes," Josephine argued.

"Look, Miss. You don't know what you're talking about. I told you —"

"Do not raise your voice to me. See,

33

Father? He is a quack. And a rude, arrogant thief."

David's temples throbbed. "I am not a quack or a thief. You do not know anything."

"Well! I know what I saw." Josephine turned to her father. "Are you going to let him talk to me this way? He deserves to be . . . to be run out of town."

"Run me out of town? Hah!" David's voice rose.

"I do not like the tone you are using to speak to my daughter. What kind of doctor are you anyway? I'm beginning to understand why you came to my office begging money. You're a slyboots, aren't you?"

David heard a chorus of gasps. The crowd was beginning to press around them. Otherwise, the room had quieted. But David's ears buzzed and bile choked his throat. "This is absurd. If only you would let me explain —"

"We'll have to ask you to leave, Sir," Mr. Caulfield said.

Where had he come from? Incredible. The host himself asking me to leave. David felt a vise latch onto his arm. A large black man propelled him forward. "Let me go!" David struggled to free himself but saw it was in vain. "All right! I'm going."

"Release him," Zachary Caulfield nodded.

34

The vise fell away from his arm. David jerked the tails of his frock coat and cast Miss Cline a furious look. She edged closer to her father, and he clutched her protectively.

"Please leave the premises," Zachary Caulfield repeated.

David clenched his jaw and strode toward the door. A path magically appeared through the crowd. The doorman held the entry door wide open. David strode through. Anger surged through him, outranked only by his burning humiliation. The last thing he heard was something muttered about "Drake's prodigy."

"Mother!" Josephine crouched over the prone woman, patting her cheek. "I'm sorry, Mother. Do come around."

Mrs. Cline raised her head. When clarity shone in her eyes, she muttered, "Randolph. Take us home."

Easily whisking her up into his arms, he looked at his daughter. "Josie?"

"I'll get our cloaks." Josie hurried to the doorman, who had their wraps already draped across his arm. She picked up bits of conversation.

"Beautiful dinner party ruined . . ."

"Exposed. A quack."

"Bravo, Miss Cline."

She hurried back to her parents, feeling more horrible by each passing minute for the scene she had caused. One more mark against her. Already she did not measure up to the etiquette rule book. Now she had argued publicly. No lady would ever do such a thing. For her own sake, her reputation didn't matter, but she hated to embarrass and disappoint her parents.

"Put me down, Randolph. I can walk." A chorus of female giggles erupted.

Josie squelched back the rising humiliation, draped her mother's cloak over her rigid shoulders, and turned to their hovering hosts. "Please accept my apologies. I do not know how to make amends."

"Yes, so sorry," Randolph Cline mumbled.

Mrs. Cline sniffed.

"Accepted. Run along and everything will be just fine. Don't you worry. A little excitement always makes a good party. Anyway, it was Drake's prodigy who caused the ruckus."

Mrs. Cline swiped away a stream of fresh tears.

Right as it had seemed to entrap Dr. Spokes — Wheeler — whatever, Josie wished she could turn back time, do things differently.

Never had such a humiliating scandal befallen David before. He hastened west, away from the Caulfield estate, wanting to put as much distance as possible between himself and the horrible Josephine Cline, the whole belittling scene. A branch scratched at his face.

"Ow!" He swiped at the night air, not breaking his stride.

An owl hooted, "Fool."

He felt the taste of blood on his lips and pressed his palm against his face. It was sticky. His foot struck something solid, and the next thing he knew, he was flailing through the blackness.

A damp cloth against David's face awakened him. The gas lantern on the nightstand hurt his eyes, and he blinked.

"There, there. Careful." Clay Buchanan's round face with its gray, bushy sideburns loomed over him.

"What happened?" David tried to rise. A pain exploded in his head, and he groaned.

"Slowly now. You know better than that."

David fought to remember. His head had hit the cobblestones, and he had looked up into a star-studded sky. But that was all.

Clay pressed the cloth against David's cheek again. "Scratched up your face. Hold still while I clean it. And you have a concussion. A fitting end to your spectacular evening, I would say." He chuckled.

"Ow!" David closed his eyes, and bits and pieces of his memory speared him between the throbs of pain in his head. Eventually he remembered the whole sorry evening. "Take me home, please."

"I don't want to move you until morning. Don't worry. Your troubles are not going anywhere. They'll still be here tomorrow." Clay chuckled again. "When you asked me the lady's name, I saw you were interested. But I sure never thought you would start a whole big row like that. What got into you anyway?"

"Me?" David raised his head again, only to feel the crashing of pain and lay back on the bed. "As you said, this can wait until morning."

The next time David opened his eyes, it was to shards of sun from a lace-curtained window. It appeared to be late morning. Slowly he lifted his head. It felt dull, but nothing like the pain he had endured the night before.

"Dr. Wheeler, I'm glad you are awake. I

was worried." He lifted his head to look at the woman who had entered the room. "Are you ready for breakfast?" Clay's servant asked.

"That sounds wonderful." David grimly remembered he had missed his dinner. As he picked through his memory, a sumptuous tray preceded the woman back into the room. He picked up the fork. "I'll be dressing next. I need to get to the clinic."

"Your clothes are there." She pointed. "But there's no need to hurry to the clinic. Mr. Buchanan went over early this morning to see to matters. He said you were to take the day off."

Swallowing a bite of fluffy eggs, David grinned at the woman. "Thank you." He had no intention of wallowing his day away. He would finish this delicious breakfast, dress, and go see what was happening at the clinic. For all he knew, there could be a whole band of respectable citizens surrounding his building, ready to take him at gunpoint down to the docks and stick him on a boat to China. China might not be such a bad idea.

That is as long as there was no one there by the name of Cline. He had all he could take of that family. Randolph Cline was a miser, only cared about his own pocket. And

Josephine? Well, she was a tigress who coldly calculated her prey, and once she had them by the throat, she savored the blood. His conscience pricked at the depths of depravity to which his thoughts were sinking. He argued with himself. *Hey, I bled, didn't I? And it was her fault. Everything was all her fault.* "Africa, maybe that's where I should go. My parents would be glad to see me."

"Excuse me? Are you speaking to me?" Clay's servant asked.

"No. I guess I was talking to myself."

She looked at the bump on his head, her expression skeptical. "Are you done with this tray?"

"Yes. Thank you." When had his life become one humiliating episode after another? And more to the point, how was he going to bring closure to this mess of misunderstandings and turn matters around? As soon as the servant was gone, he threw back the covers. He still had a headache, but his clothes went on easy enough. Now if he could just make it to the clinic.

CHAPTER 4

David dreaded what might be happening at the clinic. But when he arrived, instead of an angry mob outside, there was an eerie quiet. He opened the door. His waiting room was empty, but he heard voices coming from behind a curtain. When he drew back the canvas barrier, his assistant, Tom Langdon, looked up with surprise.

"You all right? Mr. Buchanan said you had a concussion."

"I'll explain later." Tom's patient wore a pale, strained face. His leg was exposed and bound with a tourniquet.

"Snakebite," Tom explained.

"Looks swollen." David loosened the tourniquet. "How have you treated it?"

"Bled him, was getting ready to administer a compress."

David opened his medical bag. "I've got some oak tannin here. Let's use that on the compress. Any vomiting?"

"No," the patient answered. "But my stomach feels upset. And my head is splitting. Am I going to die?"

"How long has it been?" David asked.

"A couple hours now," Tom said.

"I'm sure you'll be just fine, but we'll keep you here today just to be sure."

The man nodded. "My leg feels numb."

David finished treating the man and left the room. Tom followed. But the bell on the clinic's door jingled drawing their attention.

Clay Buchanan asked, "How's the head?"

"Better," David replied. "Thanks for taking care of me."

"I followed you last night. Thought you might need an ear. But I nearly fell over you. Found you hugging a dead hog. Surprised you didn't smell the animal."

"I was too angry."

Tom listened attentively to the other two men.

Clay waved the morning paper. "Have you seen this? Headline calls you the mumbo jumbo doctor."

Tom's eyes widened.

David swiped a hand through his hair and stared at the newspaper, dreading to hear what story had been written about last night's incident. Finally he reached out his hand. "Let me see that." *Benefit dinner ruined when mumbo jumbo doctor puts curse on woman.*

He drew his eyes closed, then opened them and frowned. "That's why the place is deserted today. She's ruined my practice."

"Nonsense. You can fight this," Clay said.

"Obviously you have not met Josephine Cline."

"I most certainly have. She's a wonderful young woman: compassionate, hardworking, very intelligent, civic-minded. . . ." His voice diminished. "Well, she is."

David glanced heavenward. "Does she by any chance have a twin sister?"

Clay chuckled. "Say, you're not in love?"

"Are you crazy? She's the kind of woman you want to stay as far away from as possible. I was considering China. Or maybe it's time to return to Africa. What am I going to do about this mess?"

"Get the paper to print a retraction. Make amends with the people you've alienated."

"That's the best you can come up with? Those men I alienated were on my list for funding the city cleanup project." He smiled sheepishly. "You're on my list, too."

"Practice on me then. Don't look so glum. You were going to make appointments with half of these people anyway. Now you have your foot in the door. It'll make for a good laugh."

"Sounds good. But you're not the one who's going to risk getting the boot."

Clay tilted his head. "On the other hand, there is another option."

"What?"

"You could let Josephine Cline get her wish. Pack up. Go abroad."

"I won't do it! But what about Randolph Cline?"

"My advice would be to stay clear of him. He dotes on his daughter."

"Naturally. Two of a kind."

"Well if you've got things under control here, I'll mosey on home."

"Thanks again, Clay. For everything."

"Think nothing of it. Only don't let me down."

David gave a reluctant nod. Clay exited. David released a weary sigh and turned to find Tom watching him. "What?" Tom quickly busied himself, and David started back to check on his only patient.

Two days passed. On the third, Randolph Cline brought home some startling news for Josie. "I ran a thorough investigation on your Dr. Spokes."

"Father, please."

44

"The results indicate that he's a young eccentric, but he's not a quack."

Josie fingered the fabric of her skirt. "But the frog."

He handed her the newspaper retraction. "The woman's illness was in her head. Wheeler tricked her, but he did it for her own good. As I said, he's not ordinary. But he has a certificate to practice medicine. He's apprenticed under Daniel Drake, and he runs a reputable clinic."

Josephine frowned at the article. "What about taking payment for trickery?"

"I don't know why he did that. Doesn't seem ethical."

"And the way he was dressed?"

"Every morning he mingles with the poor. My man followed him. It's some kind of a disguise, to blend in."

Josie felt sick. "A costume." She pressed her hands against her stomach. "What have I done?"

"Don't worry your pretty little head about it. Like I said, he's a colleague of Drake's. I don't care much for his kind. Full of crazy ideas about improving conditions of the city, social injustice. Wouldn't feel bad if we had run him off."

Furrowing her forehead, Josie considered her father's explanation. "Thank you. You've given me much to think about."

She quietly brewed over the matter for several days even though everyone else in her household deemed the incident over. Even her mother brushed the mention of it away, saying, "Trust your father, Dear. He always knows best in these matters."

And Josie tried. She really did. She even prayed about it. But the nausea and worry remained until finally she determined to make amends.

The clinic was an ordinary building from the outside. The district was not shabby or run-down exactly, yet there was nothing prestigious about it either. Josephine wondered if Dr. Wheeler had purposely chosen its location. Doctors were judged by the people they treated, affluencewise. Or was there something lacking in the doctor's abilities as she had at first imagined? Something kept him here, ministering to the middle lower-class population.

She pushed the door open, and a young plumpish man looked up from a set of books. "I'm Tom Langdon, Dr. Wheeler's assistant. Have a seat, Miss. There's a wait."

"I would like to speak with Dr. Wheeler. Is he available?"

"Are you a patient?"

"I need to see the doctor." Josephine nodded. "I'll wait my turn. Is he always this busy?"

"Sometimes." The young man leaned forward. His cheeks went pink. "There was a bit of a scandal about the doctor, and the clinic was empty for a couple days. But it was all just a rumor some woman made up. Dr. Wheeler's on the up and up. Anyway, I think everyone who was sick was holding off until they realized that, and now they all showed up at once."

Josephine felt her cheeks warm. "I hope he is as good as you claim." On the wall above a bookcase was a framed medical certificate. Josie inspected it, then seated herself. Tom Langdon left her and disappeared behind one of the curtained sections. Across the room, behind the desk where the doctor's assistant had been sitting, was a row of shelves containing jars of human organs and a skull. Why did doctors have to display such gory specimens? Crossing her arms, she planned what she would say to Dr. Wheeler and wondered how he would respond to her presence.

A male patient soon appeared from one of the curtained areas. He nodded at her and passed before he exited the clinic. After that the assistant poked his head out from behind the curtain. "You may have this room, Miss."

Josie went into the narrow room with only two solid walls. Much was crammed into the tiny area with a table taking up one entire end. On it were a microscope, a stack of papers, an array of splints, medicine, ointments, and a jar of leeches. Another table occupied the center of the room. Once the assistant left, Josie, feeling impish, hoisted herself up onto that table. A series of groans sounded from the other side of the curtain. Next she recognized the doctor's voice.

Mrs. Patterson rubbed the small of her back to show Dr. Wheeler where the pain was located.

"Here?" he asked, prodding the spot.

"Ah, that's it."

David felt the hard stays of a corset and frowned. "How long has this been hurting?"

"About a month."

"Could you walk across the room and back, please?" He watched as Mrs. Patterson's high-topped boots clapped the floorboards. Her hip jutted out more on the left side. "Mm-hmm. I see the problem."

"You do? Can you cure it?"

"No, but you can."

The woman's chin tipped upward. "What

do you mean?"

"Sit down and let me explain." Mrs. Patterson eased into a chair. "You have reached a crucial time in your life. The first signs of back pain. You have two choices. You can remedy the situation, and since this has only been hurting about a month, hopefully the pain will gradually leave until you are back to normal. Or you can continue as you are until the pain is unbearable and the problem is irreparable."

"Well!" she huffed. "Of course I wish to remedy the situation. Otherwise I would not have come to your clinic today."

"It's very simple really. Only most women object."

"Quit with the riddles, Doctor."

"Get rid of the corset."

"Why! I never!" Mrs. Patterson's face reddened.

"You must carefully consider whether you wish to be free of pain or fashionable. The corset is contrary to the way the body is designed to function. I am counting on women like you to spread the truth. We must put an end to this harmful tradition. Do you have the courage to join me in this new healthy manner of living?"

Mrs. Patterson carefully considered his recommendation. After a moment, when her face had returned more to its original hue, she said, "I do believe you are right, Doctor. My corset is going into the hearth."

"Good. And let me tell you a secret." Mrs. Patterson leaned close to him, and David whispered into her ear. "Your husband will love it."

"Oh, Doctor."

"Try this treatment and return in two weeks to report your progress."

David backed out of Mrs. Patterson's compartment and pulled back the curtain to the adjoining room. He turned. The canvas went limp in his hands. Josephine Cline challenged him with her brown gaze. He had to squelch the urge to flee. But as he stood motionless, little nudges of reason worked their way into his consciousness. *Now's your chance to clear up past misunderstandings. She's only flesh and blood, nothing worse.* He jerked the curtain closed behind him and faced his adversary.

"Miss Cline. What can I do for you?"

"I have this pain in my stomach. Sometimes in my head."

David scrutinized her. "Is this another one of your games?"

"Aren't you going to ask me when it started, as you do your other patients?"

50

"So I can add eavesdropping to your misdeeds?"

She shrugged. "The walls are thin. Go on. Ask me when it started."

David crossed his arms. "When did your symptoms start, Miss Cline?"

"The moment I learned the truth about you. I've felt horrible ever since."

"And this truth is?"

Josie jumped off her perch and gave her skirts a yank where they had caught on the edge of the table. "I am trying to apologize."

David shrugged. "It is something, I suppose. Although the damage caused by your accusations is probably irreparable."

"You could have told me what you were up to."

"Why? I don't even know you."

"I may have been wrong about your medical background. But I wasn't wrong about you. I still believe you are an arrogant, pompous man."

As the heat crept along the top of David's ears and over his brow, he realized that he was losing control of the situation again, heaping coal on the lady's boiler engine. And she had been right about one thing. The walls were thin. If he didn't calm her down, she would run off any patients that he still had. Ignoring the mounting irritation he felt and intentionally softening his tone, he said, "Forgive me for my rudeness. You caught me by surprise. Can we take this discussion elsewhere? Perhaps I can buy you dinner?"

"What?" She stared at him as if he had just eaten a mouse or done some-thing equally outrageous.

"I have patients waiting, but I also want to get this matter straightened out. Now that the shock of seeing you is over, I believe I can behave like a gentleman. How about the Emerald Inn? I can pick you up around seven o'clock."

"No."

"Miss Cline —"

"I will meet you there."

He cocked his brow. "Oh? Tonight then?"

With a nod and flurry of skirts and petticoat, Josephine agreed and disappeared.

Relief washed over David to be rid of her. But quickly following came a dread of what the evening had yet to hold. He stared at the jar of leeches across the room. He certainly was not arrogant or pompous. But he supposed he had behaved badly.

CHAPTER 5

By six o'clock, David felt as if he had caught Miss Cline's symptoms. His queasy stomach and dull head reminded him of his meetings with Vernon Thorpe and Quinton Wallace. But both of those meetings had turned out fine. Only Zachary Caulfield had not forgiven him yet. Clay Buchanan had correctly predicted that the publicity he had received at the benefit dinner incident would indirectly benefit his cause. Still, tonight was a different matter. He wished he could somehow get out of his dinner date with the explosive Miss Cline.

Still dressed in his clinic clothes, he sat sprawled, his legs stretched out in front of him. One arm dangled down, and he stroked the cat's head. "Gratuity, what if this is another one of her games? What if Randolph Cline shows up instead? Or a policeman?" His tone cheered. "Maybe she will not show up at all." But something told him that he would not be so fortunate.

"Mew."

"Time already?" As if facing the executioner, David rose. He checked his hair against a mirror and put on his top hat. The moment he opened the door, Gratuity whisked out without a backward glance. "Thanks for the moral support," he shouted after her.

Several minutes early, he secured a table inside the green, ornately trimmed restaurant and put on his professional face — the one he used when dealing with incorrigible patients.

He felt her presence the moment she entered the room. Or did he smell her? *Lavender.* Now he remembered how the soft flowery scent always enveloped her. Its fragrance had lingered in his clinic for several minutes after she had left. It wasn't a bad smell, though he preferred the stringent odors at the clinic.

The waiter ushered her toward him. David sprang up, his chair grating across the floorboards, and waited. "Good evening, Miss Cline. Please, have a seat." He turned to the waiter. "Give us a moment, please?"

"Yes, Sir."

Josephine gave David a tremulous smile. She seemed vulnerable. *Impossible.* He smiled back. "Shall we place our orders before we begin a discussion? I would recommend the pork."

"Spoken like a true citizen of Porkopolis," Josephine said.

Once the waiter had taken their orders, David tapped a long forefinger on the table. "You were right. I should have explained my behavior to you that first day. I also detest frauds. You injured my pride. Perhaps, like you say, I am arrogant."

Josie sighed. "If you can entertain the thought, you probably are not. My pride was also wounded." She looked down at her lap. "Every time I think about how you were tossed out of Mr. Caulfield's dinner, I feel sick." She met his gaze again. "I'm sorry."

"Let's put it behind us." She nodded, but David could see she was not ready to do that. "Something more troubles you?"

"Do you really go out looking for patients in the . . ."

"Slums. You can say the word." When a flush crept up her neck to her face and her eyes took on that familiar brown snappish glint, David realized it was true. He was arrogant. "Forgive me. I have this problem. I go out of my way to cater to the poor, the disabled, and the elderly; but to the young, the beautiful, and the rich I am hard, crass, and —"

"Boorish."

"Er, rather."

"So you do put on a shabby costume and go down to the slums?"

"Yes. And I won't apologize for that. I love doing it."

Her gaze softened, reminding him of the brown leather cover on his Bible. Something about it was endearing. Her voice softened as well. "I do, too."

For a moment he had to struggle to comprehend their conversation. "I seem to remember a velvet cloak and a blue silk gown."

Her eyes sparked again. "Not literally. I want to help the poor, put an end to social injustice. I want to do all those things that Father despises you for."

"I shall sleep better tonight knowing your father's low opinion of me."

She chuckled. Her laughter had a musical lilt. Their food came. After awhile, Josephine tilted her head, fascinating him with her spattering of freckles. Usually her face had been too blushed — either from anger or embarrassment — for them to shine through. She asked, "Why did you accept Mrs. Schroeder's payment?"

"Most people do not like to receive charity. It's insulting."

"That's nonsense. Why I'm a member of several charitable societies."

"Is that a fact? And you've met the recipients then?"

"Well, no. But I know from others who have that the things they receive are appreciated."

"Perhaps they are needed. Medical treatment is needed. But it destroys a person's self-respect to have to accept charity. It restores a person's dignity to pay a fair price for services or products. That's why I take whatever kind of payment they offer. I do not require it, but I accept it. There's a difference. I'm not a thief."

The freckles disappeared again. "I understand your reasoning but do not necessarily agree that people always feel that way about getting their needs met."

"When I first went into practice, I offered to donate my time. Dr. Drake warned me that I'd be better received taking a modest payment for my services. I soon learned he was right, although I should have known better just by watching my folks."

"Father says that the needy should be glad for whatever they get."

David felt a prick of anger over Randolph Cline's perception of things. It was a pity that his daughter seemed to be following in his footsteps.

"What did you mean about your folks?" she asked.

"They were missionaries. I have learned to apply some of the same principles that they used in interacting with the natives in my dealings with . . ."

"Folks from the slums? Trouble saying the word, Doctor?"

"Has anyone ever told you that you have an impertinent tongue?"

She smiled. "No, but someone did allude to something about an unbridled insulting mouth."

David pushed away his plate. "A very pretty one also. It's been a pleasure, Miss Cline. May I walk you home?"

"No, thank you. The slate is clean? Between us?"

"Spotless."

"I'll be on my way then. Thank you for the dinner. It was enlightening and very gracious of you to suggest it."

He watched her depart. Such a tiny waist. She must wear one of those ridiculous corsets. Though he doubted its necessity. After she was gone, the fragrance of lavender still lingered. David scrunched his forehead trying to remember what the medicinal value of lavender was. Ah, to relax. To relieve nervous tension. How ironic. He found it titillating.

The following morning was Saturday, and the Clines always breakfasted together on that particular day of the week before they left to go their separate ways. Normally, Josie and her father used the time to discuss some interesting topic. Today she could not get Dr. Wheeler out of her mind.

"Father, what makes a person eccentric?"

"Stubbornness. They refuse to accept the normal rules of propriety, do not fit in with society, so forth."

"You think it's a negative thing then?"

"Of course. Don't you?"

"I suppose."

"If everyone just did what they felt like doing rather than conforming to the rules laid out by society, whatever that society — a city, a business, a family — then the world would be chaotic. Don't you see, Josie?"

"But what if that eccentricity really helps others? What if a person's actions only seem outrageous because they are uncommon in that the average person does not possess enough courage to perform them? For instance — say someone has a particular need. The eccentric person, putting his own needs aside, risks ridicule or danger in an effort to help meet that other person's need. Could worry that we might be called upon to duplicate such a selfless life lead us to say the action was abnormal or eccentric when really it was brave?"

Randolph peered at her over his tea. "Are you thinking about that doctor again?"

"Perhaps I am."

"All right. Let's consider him. He makes the perfect example. Here's a man who could spend his time treating the sick. When one has a diploma and a clinic, wouldn't you think that taking care of the sick people would be the thing he should do? But, no. Instead, he wants to hire immigrants to sweep the city clean of refuse. Only he doesn't want to use his money. No. He comes to me and asks me to fund his ridiculous idea. Then he threatens me by saying my family will die of cholera if I don't. Now, that's eccentric. And there's not a good thing about it."

Josie was amazed. "He threatened us with cholera?"

"He certainly did. Made me feel like it was all my fault that the city has problems."

"Do not talk about that disease in this house," Mrs. Cline clipped. "I shall not allow it."

"Sorry, Dear," Mr. Cline said. "I did get carried away, didn't I?"

"Sorry, Mother," Josie dittoed.

"Apology accepted. Now let's talk about something pleasant."

Everyone studied their eggs and bacon, trying to come up with a topic.

"Did you know that the orphanage has doubled since it opened its doors? Now that's a good thing, isn't it?" Mrs. Cline asked.

Josie blinked. She knew her mother meant well.

"All those poor children," Mrs. Cline murmured. "See how fortunate you are, Josie?"

Josie blotted her mouth with her cloth napkin to keep from smiling. "Yes, Mother." The room grew quiet again, and Josie remembered Dr. Wheeler's claim that people didn't like to receive charity. She wished to test his theory. "Mother, what are you doing today? Would you like to go with me to visit Mrs. Schroeder?"

"Why I suppose I could."

"Do you think we could take one of those comforters you made?"

Mrs. Cline's eyes lit. "Oh, yes. Let's."

Randolph Cline pushed away from the

table. "You ladies be careful. Take the carriage."

"I'd rather walk, Father. It's not far."

"But your mother —"

"If Josie recommends it, I'm certainly courageous enough."

Mr. Cline covered his smile in his napkin. "Well, I suppose . . ."

Mrs. Cline pecked her husband on the cheek. "Don't you have a land deal or something to attend to?"

"I can take a hint." He picked up his topper. "Good day, ladies."

"Bye, Father."

As soon as he was gone, Josie turned to her mother. "Let's go pick out a comforter. I'm sure Mrs. Schroeder will be most appreciative."

CHAPTER 6

Josie slowed her pace to match her mother's as they started toward the canal that cut horizontally through their city. Glancing over, Josie asked, "How do you feel?"

"This walking does me good. My back was a bit stiff this morning. I believe it is all the sewing that I do."

Josie leaned close so Charles couldn't hear. "Have you ever considered going without a corset? I hear it helps the back."

"You sound just like your father."

So there *was* something that Dr. Wheeler and Father agreed upon. Josie bit back a smile. They passed rows of rectangular blocks of houses and the occasional conspicuous mansion.

The first of autumn's leaves made the cobblestones crunchy. Squashing the brown and yellow bits of beech, poplar, and hickory beneath her boots, she prayed. *Lord, why does this man intrigue me so?* She lifted her gaze upward. Gilded church spires speckled the horizon. Overhead, fluffy clouds sailed by. God's presence was subtle yet all encompassing.

Man's presence was also evident. Smoke poured from chimneys of the steam foundries. Behind them, steamboats hissed past Cincinnati's busy quay on the Ohio River. And when they reached the canal, the stench of decaying animal flesh overpowered the fresh scent of autumn.

Josie looked over her shoulder before crossing the canal. "How are you doing, Charles?"

The immigrant boy peeked from around the bundle of comforter. "Fine I am, Miss Cline."

They crossed, and soon Josie recognized Mrs. Schroeder's building. Upon their last visit Charles had informed her it was the one by the sausage man. "Here it is, Mother." She rushed forward and opened the side door. They climbed the steps to the third floor, and Josie knocked.

Mrs. Schroeder's face broke into a smile as soon as she recognized Josie and saw her son. She motioned them in and rattled off a string of foreign words.

Charles was crushed in his mother's embrace, unable to reciprocate with the bundle in his arms.

"Tell her that we would like her to have the comforter, Charles," Josie urged.

Josie watched mother and son converse.

Josie watched the woman's expressions change and wondered what was being said. She was able to relax when Mrs. Schroeder chuckled, put her arm around her son's shoulder, and motioned for Charles to place the comforter on the bed. The next thing she knew, they were being led to a small table. Josie and her mother took the only two chairs, and Mrs. Schroeder brought out an apple dish and made them a pot of tea.

"What is this?" Mrs. Cline asked.

"Strudel," Charles replied. "Is *gut.*"

Josie felt very guilty taking the woman's food, but Dr. Wheeler's explanation about accepting payment helped her to enjoy the light meal. It tasted scrumptious, melting in her mouth.

When they rose to leave, Charles translated the farewells and said that he would catch up with them.

"Father will have your hide if you do not," Josie warned, then led her mother down the stairs and back outside. Another pang of guilt accosted her, this time from remembering how she had chased after Dr. Wheeler, hurling her insults. Amends were made, she reminded herself. She must put it behind her.

"That was so rewarding, wasn't it, Dear?" Mrs. Cline asked on the walk home.

"Yes, but the money Mrs. Schroeder received for Charles's apprenticeship will not sustain her forever. She's going to have to get a job."

"Maybe the women's workhouse can find her something. That reminds me; I've got to find someone to replace Dr. Fitch. He was scheduled to hold a clinic for the women but got called away because of family concerns. I could ask Dr. Cook, but he's so crotchety."

"I know the perfect person for your clinic. Dr. Wheeler."

"Now, Josephine, how can you say such a thing? After all the trouble that man caused."

"I caused the trouble. He told me that it's his life's work to care for the poor."

"When did he tell you that?"

Josie did not want to admit that she had met with the doctor. "When we spoke, of course. And Father told me where his clinic is. I'll ask him if you wish."

"I don't know what your father would say about it."

"Let me handle Father, and consider it

done. Now, about Mrs. Schroeder getting a job: Do you think we should discuss it with Charles?"

"What to ask me?" panted the young man.

Josie turned. "Charles! What are you doing with that comforter? You were supposed to leave that with your mother."

Mrs. Cline wheeled about. "Oh, no. Didn't you understand that was a gift for your mother?"

His shoulders stiffened. "This kind she does not use. German feather covers she likes."

Josie fingered the puffy cloth. Her voice saddened. "She rejected our gift?"

"To you, we thank."

"Well, Josephine. There are plenty of others who might use this comforter." Mrs. Cline's voice was prickly.

"Are there, Mother?"

The older woman's voice softened. "There is always the orphanage."

Josie felt a rush of tears and pinched the bridge of her nose. "Charles, would you like me to carry it for awhile?"

"No, Miss Cline. Fine I am."

David grimaced, then continued to clean the decaying skin tissue surrounding the snakebite. He reapplied a compress and

67

bandage.

"Looks nasty. Doesn't it, Doc?"

"Did you stay off your leg like I advised?"

"Not entirely."

"This is a serious matter. Some folks die from snakebite. You don't want to lose your foot, do you?"

"You didn't tell me I could lose my foot."

"How did you get here?"

His patient looked at the floor. "Walked."

"I was afraid of that. I'll have my assistant take you home. You are to stay off this leg until I tell you different. I'll come out to your place morning after next."

"I'd appreciate that. And I'll stay in bed. I promise."

"But if it looks any worse, you get word to me, and I'll be out sooner."

The patient nodded. "Yes, Doc. Thank you."

David swiped an arm across his brow and opened the curtain to his next patient. His stride broke. "Miss Cline?" He eyed her carefully. "What brings you back to the clinic?"

Josephine slid down off the table, her skirts swishing around her ankles. "Dr. Wheeler, I need your help. Oh, don't raise your eyebrow at me. Did you know you have a habit of doing that?"

"No, I didn't. What kind of help?"

"Mother volunteers at the women's work-house. It is a society which finds jobs for women and meets various needs."

"I'm aware of the organization. Go on."

"We were wondering if you would be able to hold a clinic. There goes that brow again. It's quite intimidating, you know."

He doubted that anything could intimidate Miss Cline. "When?"

"At your convenience. You did mention that you had a heart for the poor, the —"

"I remember what I said. How about Friday? I could be available from noon on."

"Perfect. Mother will be so happy."

"But I have a condition. Now you're doing it. The eyebrow thing."

"I am not. Am I?"

"Very prettily, too."

Josephine's face reddened. "What is your condition, Doctor?"

"That you serve as my assistant."

"But you have an assistant. Tom Langdon. Can't you bring him?"

"Tom will need to cover here. Sorry, that's my condition."

"But I know nothing about medicine." Her gaze flittered around the room. "Do you think I'm capable?"

"I do."

Josie stepped forward and held out her hand. "Very well. It's a deal."

David shook the small gloved hand and sealed their agreement. "I'm looking forward to it." Her gaze softened, and David suddenly felt uncomfortable in a nice sort of way. He broke away from her gaze and asked in a rather gruff voice. "Have they held clinics before?"

"Yes."

"I guess they'll know what needs to be done to prepare."

"I'll check with Mother and let you know if she has any questions."

"I'm curious, Miss Cline. Does your father know about this?"

"No, Dr. Wheeler. He does not."

"Do you think you should tell him?"

"He says you are eccentric. I'm sure he would not approve."

David wondered if Miss Cline also thought he was eccentric. Of course she must. But there was something else in her gaze that held approval. Why not? Wasn't Miss Cline a bit of a bluestocking? "Ordinary" was probably not even in her vocabulary.

"On Friday then," she was saying.

David strode forward and pulled back the curtain for her. "Miss Cline?"

She paused. "Yes?"

"The next time you call, you have merely to tell my assistant you wish to speak with me. You do not need to wait until it's your turn as if you were a patient."

"Are you sure? He has not been very co-operative in the past."

"I'll speak with him."

"No, thank you. I'll take care of it, Doctor. Good day."

David watched her depart. She stopped in front of Tom. "Why does he keep such gory things in his office?" she asked.

"To impress his patients," Tom answered with a blush on his plump cheeks.

David could not hear her reply after that, but whatever she said, it made Tom smile. Did she always cause a stir — dazzling, infuriating, affecting in some way everyone she met? She had certainly turned his world upside down. He had never wanted to see her again, had even contemplated China. Now she seemed to have him at her beck and call.

It was as if she felt his eyes upon her back, because just before she exited the clinic, she turned around and gave him a little wave. David gave her a stiff nod, feeling the heat rush up his neck and face. Tom shook his head as if he understood, then asked their snakebite patient. "You ready to go?"

Jerking his gaze away from the door, David pulled back the adjoining curtain.

CHAPTER 7

On Friday David easily recognized Mrs. Cline, remembering her from the Caulfields' benefit dinner — the one he wished he could blot from his memory. From her expression, Mrs. Cline seemed to also recall the events of that calamitous evening. Josephine had not mentioned that her mother held ill feelings toward him, but it was only logical that she might, for both women lived under Randolph Cline's influence.

As she approached him, she tilted her head slightly as if she studied an enigma. But her voice was pleasant. "So kind of you to come, Dr. Wheeler."

"I am happy to oblige."

She turned to retrace her steps. "If you will follow me, I will show you where to set up your clinic."

They passed a large open workroom where a group of women unraveled short lengths of rope. David was familiar with the

73

procedure of removing the oakum for use in caulking ship seams. Others were busy with sewing projects. Several cast him curious looks. He and Mrs. Cline rounded a corner. Already a line of women had formed.

"Here we are. Let me know when you've finished attending to the sick. I'll send you some new applicants to determine if they are able-bodied or infirm."

David addressed the women waiting in line as they passed. "I need a minute to prepare." Nods and murmurs followed. Then he thanked Mrs. Cline.

"Josephine should be along shortly."

"Good. Her help will be appreciated. I like to have another female present in situations like this."

Mrs. Cline departed, and David laid out his instruments and medicine. The reason he had given her for asking for Josephine's assistance was not the only reason. His curiosity had not been satiated regarding her. It would be a good test of her character — setting her up in a situation where she would be called upon to respond to the needs of others. He supposed he judged everyone by this standard though he knew it was not fair to do so. Every person had their own niche in life. Even so, he had to know if Josephine would meet his particular expectations.

The door opened. Josephine wore a gray wool dress. It was very becoming. Practical. He liked it.

"Looks like we'll have a busy afternoon."

"Hello, Miss Cline. I hoped you would come."

"I promised, didn't I? What can I do to help?"

"You may admit our first patient."

This was a middle-aged, reed-thin woman with a burdensome cough. First, David put on his stethoscope and listened to the woman's frail chest. Next, he poured some medicine in a spoon, instructing Josephine to administer the dosage. As he prepared a small bottle for the woman to take with her when she left, Josephine spoke soothingly to the woman, even eliciting a smile from the drawn face.

David drew Josephine aside. "She needs nourishment. Can the workhouse provide a hearty soup for her and any of the others whom I designate?"

"I'm sure they can. I'll go make arrangements if you like."

"Yes. Take her along and see that she is cared for. But please hurry back. I need you."

Josephine smiled. "I will."

Turning back to the woman, he said, "You need to eat well and rest until this cough is gone. Miss Cline will see that both are arranged."

The woman left with Josephine. David admitted the next patient who was pregnant but appeared healthy.

He examined her and two others before Josephine returned. "Just write down the names of the women who need food, some other special item, or time off work. Their addresses are on file, and it will be taken care of," she said.

"Good. Thank you. I should have asked about that before we got started."

"Mother apologizes for not giving you the information. She admits that she was distracted. Rather intrigued with you."

"Oh?"

"Your name did come up at our dinner table after the night of our . . . incident."

"She must trust your judgment to allow me to step into this facility."

"I hadn't thought about it that way. I guess I did put her on the spot. But I think she likes you."

David felt intrigued by the way Miss Cline's voice softened when she admitted it, almost as if it mirrored her own feelings.

But Miss Cline was not one to hold back her thoughts. If she felt that way, she would just say so. And she hadn't. It occurred to him that while he had subconsciously been subjecting Miss Cline to testing, she was probably doing the same to him. He wondered if he would pass her inspection. Probably no one could ever score high enough to compete with her father.

"I appreciate your mother's open-minded spirit. Now let's admit the next patient."

The line finally dwindled, and the new applicants were also examined. Well after dark, Miss Cline sank into a chair and rested the side of her face in the cup of her hand. "I'm exhausted. How do you do this every day?"

"Not every day is this busy. Can I hail a hackney for you or walk you home?"

"Yes, but let me help you clean up first so that we can both leave."

Not lacking in Miss Cline's demeanor was perseverance. He liked that. In fact, he hadn't found anything negative about their teamwork. It seemed that she was not going to disappoint him after all.

Outside the women's workhouse, David held up a gas lamp. The bleak brick building with its dreary stone wall loomed behind them. No hackney was within sight. He hated to send her back inside again. "I'll have to hunt one down for us."

"Wait." She lightly touched his forearm. "That's too much trouble. I'll just walk home."

David gazed down the dark street, not knowing how long it would take to locate a hackney. "Only if you allow me to escort you, Miss Cline. It's the least I can do. I wouldn't have made it today without your help. I'd still be working, and women would still be lined —"

"Yes. That would be nice. But please, call me Josephine."

He offered the support of his arm, and she took it. At first they walked in silence. The lantern provided light for their path and was especially helpful when they encountered a new construction area and found it necessary to dodge bricks and trash.

"Careful. This litter is so dangerous," he said.

"The city is expanding rapidly. That is a good thing. Father's business is booming."

Besides being in the textile business, Mr. Cline was a land developer. Quite possibly the materials strewn across the way were results of his very own projects. David could barely hold back his contempt for the sloppy conditions.

"Father would have come for me himself tonight, but he was taking a steam bath."

David stiffened.

"Did I say something wrong?"

"You are perceptive. Are you sure you want to hear my opinion?"

Her voice took on an edgy quality. "About my father?"

"About steam baths."

"Oh. What about them?"

"There's nothing harmful about them, but they're not beneficial either. I'd categorize them under leisure and relaxation. And please do not tell me that your father imbibes lobelia."

"But it is highly recommended for many ailments. A friend of Father's introduced him to its beneficial qualities."

"Zero. That's its medicinal value. I suppose he also takes the waters."

Josephine withdrew her hand. "I do not like your tone of voice."

"I'm sorry, but I believe that you should learn the proper use for the word *quack*."

With that, she released an unfeminine grunt and hastened her pace away from him.

Realizing that she would most likely stumble and injure herself if she did not walk within the lantern's circle of light, David hurried after her, grabbing her arm. "Josephine, wait."

She jerked away and continued to walk. The lantern picked up some new structures, and he grabbed her arm again, "Look out. Stop."

Definitely angry now, Josephine stopped and whirled to face him. Her lips were firmly pressed together; her freckles stood out against her white face.

"I'm sorry," David said. "I didn't realize I was full of all that hostility. I . . . Please, forgive me."

She gave one nod but kept her distance from him as they commenced to walk. Silence invaded the blackness. David cleared his throat. "I worked beneath Dr. Drake. He is a marvelous physician. His genius far exceeds the medical field. He's been opposing the practices and the whole theory of steam and lobelia. It's something we feel so strongly about. I'm sorry I made it personal."

Silence continued to pervade, except for the sounds of boots on cobblestones and the rustling and chirps of night. David remembered the meeting in Mr. Cline's office and that Josephine's father had looked as if he had been experiencing pain. "How is your father's health?"

"He has some problems. But I'd rather

not talk about them."

"All right. I don't suppose he would accept my help anyway."

"You are correct on that account. Well, Doctor, my street is just ahead. I can make it fine on my own now."

"I'll see you to your door."

"As you wish."

The silence prevailed, but the houses loomed larger. In Cincinnati, it was commonplace for the mansions and normal-sized houses to be mixed. As they approached the Cline residence, David felt as if a fist squeezed his heart. Any hopes he might have entertained about friendship with Josephine fled when he realized which house she claimed as her own. It was one he had oftentimes admired. It was outlandish and completely out of his class. It only solidified how wide the ravine was between him and the Clines.

"Here we are." Josephine turned toward him. She sounded as if her anger had finally subsided. "Thank you for everything. The clinic. Seeing me home."

"It has been my pleasure. If there is anything I can do to help again, I am at your service."

"Good evening," she said in a dejected tone.

He understood. It matched his feelings. The gulf between them was so vast, yet there was a part of him that wished he could explore the mystery of Josephine Cline.

As he walked home, he went over their past encounters. Every single time he saw her, he had been strongly affected. True, most often it had been adversely; still, she remained a challenge dangled in front of him. The challenge presented was to explore the many facets of this woman's explosive personality. Yet with every encounter he had discovered areas of contention.

She had not passed his test after all. He felt like a teacher who hated to give the low mark. Disappointment and sadness loomed darker than the night. And so he picked his way home. At least Gratuity would be there waiting, glad to see him. His stomach growled. He needed to eat something though he didn't know what to fix. Food and a good night's rest. Then he would feel better.

Oftentimes he felt this way after helping patients with illnesses that were painful or fatal. The only comfort he could find at such times was in his faith in God. The worn, brown leather Bible that waited on his bed appealed to him even more than a meal. His steps quickened.

CHAPTER 8

All things are full of labour, David read to himself, then said, "Listen to this, Gratuity. The king and writer of Ecclesiastes felt just like I do. 'The eye is not satisfied with seeing' — bodies weakened with sickness and pain — 'nor the ear filled with hearing' — rattling coughs, fears of the aged, unfulfilled dreams."

"Meow."

"You, too, eh?" *Weary. That pretty well sums It up. I am weary.* Ever since he had gone to the clinic at Josephine's request two weeks earlier, his spirit was depressed. The melancholy that had struck him outside the Clines' opulent residence had settled in and nested. His outlook was as bleak as the chill that had swept through the city, bringing with it the onset of sickness.

"Tonight there's a lecture on Indian land treaties. Dr. Drake suggested I attend. Maybe he's right. I'm not stretching my mind enough. I need to rise above this, somehow."

"Meow."

"You're not going to another lecture, Josie," her mother scolded. "About next the young men will be calling you a bluestocking."

"They already are, and you very well know it. But I don't care. That just shows how shallow men are these days. All except Father, of course. And he is looking forward to our attending it together."

"I suppose . . . Perhaps I should have a talk with him about dragging you to these functions."

"Nonsense. Ready, Darling?"

"Yes, Father." Josephine placed a juicy kiss on her mother's cheek. "Don't worry, Mother. It will give you wrinkles."

Mrs. Cline smiled. "Oh, run along then. Both of you."

"Sure you don't want to join us?" Mr. Cline asked, giving her a squeeze.

"No. I've got some sewing. Maybe next time I'll go."

Josie and her father chuckled all the way to the carriage over that possibility. They were among the last to arrive and slipped quietly into two vacant seats near the back. The speaker had already taken his place and announced his topic, Indian land treaties.

Since Tecumseh died in the War of 1812 and his brother The Prophet more recently, Ohio has been at peace. But only because of mass Indian removal, and now new treaties are being signed to take away Indian land.

Josie listened attentively until her eyes meandered over the backs of the men and women between her and the speaker and snagged upon a particular set of shoulders. She studied the man, wishing he would turn so she could see if it was David.

A coughing spell from across the room caught his attention. He turned sideways. It was Dr. Wheeler. What a lovely opportunity with such a perfect line of vision to discreetly scrutinize the man who was even more fascinating than the lecture. His face was lean and pleasant. She wondered why she had not noticed before how incredibly handsome he was. His hat was off, revealing a shock of wavy blond hair parted on the side and full above the ears. Sideburns a darker shade of blond lined his jaw and became one with the even darker beard that encircled his fine chiseled chin.

His blue eyes looked concerned. She had

to admire the way the physician in him always oozed out. She imagined that he was mentally diagnosing and would not be surprised to see him rise and cross the room to treat the man with the coughing spell.

The sick man rose and hurried outside. Heads turned. The speaker hesitated until the room quieted again, then continued. And not to disappoint her, Dr. Wheeler rose and followed the man outside, black bag in hand. He was the most stubborn and opinionated man she'd ever met, but at least his heart was in the right place.

What a coincidence that he should be in attendance. Ever since she had helped him at the clinic and they had argued, she had tried to put him out of her mind. He was trouble — had been from the start. But she had not been able to dismiss him, and the more she had thought about him and their last discussion, the easier it had been to forgive him for it. Not because she agreed with him, but because she could sympathize with him and understand why he felt so strongly about the steam baths.

And now, just seeing him stirred up that strange longing that she always felt regarding him. It must be her natural curiosity. Father said it was a good thing. Mother thought it was part of the reason she was still single at twenty-two. For Josie it only kept life interesting.

The doctor reappeared and took his seat again. Josie felt her heartbeat quicken. This handsome intriguing man aroused unexplainable desires. She began to imagine what a friendship with him might be like. But how could she get close when he displayed such an indifferent attitude toward her?

Although the plight of the Indians interested her, she could not wait until the lecture was finished, and finally it did come to an end. But before she could reach the doctor, he was headed for the door. She grabbed up her skirts and hurried after him.

"Dr. Wheeler." His back visibly stiffened. He turned, and she gave him her most engaging smile, determined to penetrate his aloof exterior. "It is so good to see you again."

"Josephine, I am surprised. I did not notice you in the crowd."

"You sat in my line of vision. You look tired. Your practice must be busy."

He shrugged. "Just the usual. But I have felt a bit tired."

"Perhaps you need a diversion."

He smiled. "That's why I came tonight."

She plunged ahead, briefly touching his

coat sleeve. "There is a new exhibit at the Western museum. I was planning to go see it next week."

"We go about in different circles, Josephine."

"Nonsense. We are both here tonight, aren't we? Will you be my escort?" The doctor studied her. She felt the heat rise up her neck. "And please, do not cock your brow at me."

He smiled. "If I refuse, you will probably do something dreadful. Something my practical brain cannot even conjure up. It's frightening. I have learned from past experience, when the lady speaks, I need to listen."

"It is settled then. You can pick me up at one o'clock on Saturday. Be prepared. I intend to present you to Father. Here he comes now. Be off, and I'll see you next week."

The doctor chuckled and shook his head at her before he ducked out the door, and she felt a little taste of victory.

"Was that your Dr. Spokes?" Randolph asked.

"Why, yes it was. He's a very fascinating man. In fact, he is taking me to the Western museum next Saturday.

"I do not like it, Josie."

"Please, Father. Don't cause a scene."

Randolph frowned. "We'll talk about him later."

David almost wished he had his melancholy back. At least it had been consistently reliable and had not interfered with his work. Instead, after seeing Josephine again, for the remainder of the week he had been on an emotional seesaw. The highs were: Josephine was healthy, fresh, revitalizing. Spring in the middle of autumn. His days were not so monotonous, but rather they were filled with anticipation of what their next encounter might bring. No doubt when they attended the museum together, their outing would include another lively discussion.

But when the seesaw dipped, his thoughts scraped the ground. Probably there would be a controversy, and very likely even a scene when Mr. Cline entered the picture. And even if everything went well, in the end he would get hurt. As intriguing as she was, he knew that a friendship with her would never work.

He remembered his boyhood days and how intrigued he had been with African insects. Even though he knew better, many times he had held on until he was either bitten or stung. By the end of the week, he had convinced himself that it would be better to release Josephine before the same thing happened with her. Somehow when they attended the museum together, he would convince her that it was for the best.

The hackney pulled up outside the Clines' residence, and David climbed down and went to Josephine's door. A servant admitted him and told him where to wait. It was not long before she appeared — a vision, just as she had been at the benefit dinner. Her beauty sent a foreboding feeling up his spine. He needed to put on his guard.

"You look splendid," she said.

"I believe I was supposed to say that. You are quite lovely."

"And you are fortunate this time. Father is gone."

He escorted her out and helped her into the hackney. It lurched forward.

"I never know what to expect from you," she said. "Sometimes you are dressed in rags. Other times you are the epitome of fashion."

"Let's not exaggerate, shall we?"

"You choose the topic then, Doctor."

"We can talk about fashion. Did you know that wearing a cravat too tight is unhealthy?"

"I did not. Do you suppose that styles will change to accommodate comfort?"

90

"By all means. One day we will all be wearing sacks again."

Josephine smiled. "After everyone else conforms, then maybe I shall wear a sack. I believe you would do it today if it were to help someone."

It was the way she softened her voice again that squeezed his heart. He felt his guard slipping, and he swallowed. "I believe we have arrived." The coach lurched to a stop. David opened the door and jumped down, offering her the aid of his hand. "Shall we?"

The new exhibit was full of outrageous art: a life-size painting of a maniac, an anaconda devouring a horse and rider, and Col. David Crockett grinning the opossum off a tree. As they toured the museum, Josephine was all that was charming and sweet. He knew that if he was to stick to his plans, he was going to have to speak with Josephine before she endeared herself further, or worse, before he drowned in her sea of loveliness and perfection.

"Josephine, let's leave this crowded room," he whispered. "It's not healthy to breathe in all this stuffy air."

"By all means, I commend my health into your capable hands."

They entered a room of science, and he turned to face her. "I wish you would not do this," he said.

"What? What am I doing?"

"You are being too charming for my own good. This is going nowhere."

"I do not understand."

"Us. It won't work."

"I do not intend to let you analyze our friendship with logical deductions."

"You are too late. I have already done so."

"You have weighed the pros and cons and found me wanting?"

"No. Not you. You are witty, vivacious, and dangerous. It is me. I do not have time to exert energies in such entertainments. I have aspirations, causes, very serious day-to-day issues, boring things that fill my life. I have no time for amusement and games, engaging as you are. If you respect me and care for me at all, you will honor my wishes."

"You're afraid of Father. I know that he can be quite intimidating. He knew I was coming with you tonight. Once he gets used to the idea of —"

"Oh, for pity's sake. Have you not been listening? You are . . . are lavender, and I am castor oil."

"That is the most ridiculous thing I have ever heard. I'll tell you what you are. You are a fool."

"I'm sure you are correct. Come. I will

see you home."

He was miserable. Josephine would not look at him the entire ride across town, only stared out the small window. When she finally did, her eyes were red rimmed. But he had to be strong, end it now before he really got hurt. Although he wondered how it could hurt any worse than this. He helped her out of the carriage.

She paused. "At one time I thought you were mysterious. Now I think you are dull, stupid, and insipid."

"Insipid," he murmured, after she was gone. "That's probably true. But stupid?" He climbed back in the hackney, leaned back more weary than ever, and wished he had never laid eyes on her.

CHAPTER 9

David was on his way to the hospital and had just passed the Cincinnati College when he spotted a group of young men dicing. Usually he broke up such a gang. Not only was the practice illegal, but he hated to see boys get drawn into such an addiction. Today, however, he guiltily looked aside for he was in a hurry. Across the street was Dr. Drake's eye infirmary and marine hospital. He quickly made his way into the building and down a long hall, where he knocked on a closed door.

"Come in." Drake, who greatly resembled an older version of Abraham Lincoln, looked up, his face swallowed up in his smile. "David, I heard you caused a scandal in our fine city."

David gave a grim smile. "Just a bit of a stir. How was your trip?"

"Successful enough. I'm anxious to work on the resource materials that I have collected. But let's talk about you. How's the clinic?"

David leaned forward, his elbows resting on his legs, his face cupped in his hands. "It was a bit slow with the scandal and all, but has pretty much returned to normal. My assistant, Tom Langdon, is such a help."

"You must not get too dependent upon him. Why don't you send him over here to help out at the hospital when you are not so busy. It would be good experience for him."

"I suppose I could. If you think so."

"Good. We can use him. Now, let's take a look at that list of names I gave you before I left." David withdrew it from his pocket and gave it to Dr. Drake, who summarized the results aloud. "Randolph Cline, crossed off the list. Vernon Thorpe, Quinton Wallace, and Clay Buchanan all have contributed generous sums."

David felt embarrassed that he had not done better. "I didn't make a very good showing, did I?"

"It's a start. I've done this myself plenty of times. I know it's not an easy task. That's why I gave it to you. I have confidence in you, David. This negative attitude is uncharacteristic of you."

"You're right. I'll pull up my bootstraps, Sir."

David left the hospital with a determination that wasn't there before. Dr. Drake certainly knew how to motivate. Why, just a short visit with the man made David feel like he actually could make a difference in the world, or at least in Cincinnati. Maybe even Ohio. He felt a surge of excitement that had been missing and wanted to pass it on to Tom. The boy deserved some encouragement, too.

But later that day in speaking with Tom, David discovered the young man wasn't eager about his new assignment at the hospital. David did what he could to raise Tom's spirits and kindle enthusiasm in that part of his assistant's new job assignment even though it meant more work for himself at the clinic.

In the evening, David prayed over the two remaining names on his list: Zachary Caulfield, who still had not forgiven him for ruining his benefit dinner, and Bartholomew Hastings. He prayed that by word of mouth the circle of donors would enlarge.

After that his days were packed and busy. As autumn progressed, daylight hours shortened. That, combined with Tom's time spent at the hospital, caused David to drop into bed each night exhausted.

■ ■ ■ ■

Josie peered outside her bedroom window at what remained of the cook's pumpkin patch. She felt restless as if she were on the brink of change or discovery but it was just beyond her reach. She could not tell if the feeling had made her pray more or if her frequent prayers made the nudge stronger. Her fingertip followed a stream of liquid down the frosty glass. *Lord, what are You trying to tell me?* A knock at her bedroom door interrupted her prayer. *Sorry, Lord. I guess we'll have to continue our discussion later. There's always something to take up my time. Forgive me for my bad thoughts. Help me to be agreeable.* "Yes?"

"It's Mother. May I come in?"

"Coming." Josephine fastened her wrapper and padded across the floor.

"I didn't wake you?"

"No. Come in."

They sat together on the bed. "I was wondering if you wanted to help me out at the workhouse today? One of our volunteers canceled. And I remembered how well you handled things when you assisted Dr. Wheeler's clinic."

"When are you leaving?"

Her mother looked apologetic. "Right after breakfast. It will be a long day."

Josephine gave her mother a quick hug. "Then I'd best get dressed right away."

"Thank you, Darling."

As soon as her foot crossed the threshold of the women's workhouse, vivid memories of her time spent with Dr. Wheeler accosted her — the remembrance of how he had rejected her offer of friendship. He had made it plain that she was a hindrance to his high and lofty plans. And to think she had thought him fascinating. Stubborn and unapproachable were more like it.

Certainly David Wheeler had dual sides to his personality. There was the man who dressed shabbily to better serve the poor. He was compassionate and gallant. But his other half was rude and prejudiced against the rich. Unfortunately, that was the one whose acquaintance she had made.

"Josie?"

"Yes, Mother?"

"Come let me show you the forms that need to be filled out by new applicants. You can sit at this table to help with the interviews."

First was a cane-wobbly woman, kicked out of her home because she could not walk to her job anymore. Her hands were still good, but work was unavailable. Her family was dead, and she was alone in the world. She was a perfect candidate for those who resided full time at the workhouse. Josie's heart warmed when she saw the woman's one possession — her Bible. Once the interview was ended, another workhouse resident in charge of newcomers took the sweet old woman away to get her settled in.

Josie's next candidate was quite a contrast — a young woman with a toddler in tow. She still had a home but had lost her job and needed money to pay her rent. Together they compared a list of available jobs to her qualifications. Josie was glad they could offer her a job at the textile factory. The woman only needed to obtain a letter of recommendation.

The third applicant started toward Josie when a resident burst into the room breathless. "Mrs. Cline, where's the wardress? There's a fight!"

"Oh, I do hate these," Mrs. Cline murmured, stumbling to her feet.

"I'll go find her," Josephine assured her mother and hurried after the messenger. By the time they reached the scuffle, the wardress had already arrived and broken up the fight. But the entire incident greatly affected Josie. When she returned to her mother, she asked, "What will happen to them? One of them was pregnant. And she was so young."

"They are allowed three misdemeanors. After that they must leave. The penalty is extra work or less food."

"That's horrible," Josie said. "I thought this was an institute to help women, not a penitentiary."

"You cannot help a troublemaker. They ruin things for all the others."

For the remainder of the day, Josie thought about the incident. That evening the matter still disturbed her. She prayed about it, thankful that she could go to the Lord with her problems. Where did people turn when they did not know Jesus? She tried to imagine what it might feel like to have to carry a burden all alone. The loneliness and desperation that enveloped the applicants haunted her.

It was no wonder that all that ugliness tumbled out in uncontrollable emotions causing disruptions with other innocent persons. The women at the women's workhouse carried more problems than most. They stored it up until something happened to cause them to explode or act out their frustrations — just as she had witnessed today with those two women brawling over a minor incident. She probably would have done the same thing. They could not help themselves.

Her mind scrabbled for a solution, something that might help them cope. Of course they needed to know the Lord. Then an idea struck. In awe, she thanked the Lord for it. It seemed right, but was it feasible?

David pushed back his breakfast plate of scorched eggs and stretched his legs, his gaze fastened to the morning newspaper. A hand-sketched picture drew his interest, and he straightened, carefully studying the young woman whose familiar face and name set his heart to pounding. *Josephine Cline addresses board of women's workhouse.* What was she up to now? Curious, he pulled the paper close to his face to better read the details. He shook his head in admiration and wonderment. "Listen to this, Gratuity. 'Josephine Cline's idea of assigning a personal patroness to each woman at the workhouse was readily received. Volunteers are now needed. A personal patroness would meet once a week for one hour to discuss the resident's personal problems and give advice. Although the personal patroness plan would aid individuals and head off many workhouse problems, and it cannot be denied that it is a good plan, the question remains: Can enough volunteers be found?' "

A fountain of excitement bubbled up inside him. He had been pretending these past several weeks that he had never heard of Josephine Cline, never looked into her soft, leather-brown eyes, never smelled the scent of lavender. One could do that. Suppress a thing for awhile. But not forever. It was bound to surface time and time again. The question was: What was he going to do with these tangled feelings he felt for Josephine?

The cat meowed. He needed to quit his daydreaming and get to the clinic. But tonight, if she entered his thoughts again, he would pray about the matter. Just to make certain, he left the paper lying open to her picture.

CHAPTER 10

Even though Josephine was a closed chapter of David's life, after reading the newspaper article, his fingers itched to reopen the book and explore her captivating pages. Every fiber of his being pricked with an awareness that he had missed the major point before. That he needed to reexamine the text for that missing element. Oftentimes he read a favorite book more than once, savored endings over and over. He shook his head. What was he doing comparing Josephine to a book?

She was flesh and blood and lived in a real and intimidating house. It loomed before him this very instant, tall and ominous, challenging his spontaneous idea of calling upon Josephine to congratulate her on her recent achievement.

It was only a house, after all. He knocked. The door opened, and a servant inquired of his purpose.

"I wish to call upon Miss Cline if she is available."

"And whom shall I tell her is calling?"

"David Wheeler." He stepped inside and waited in the entry while the servant left to find Josephine. The wall tapestry reminded him of the textile factory that Mr. Cline owned shares in. He hoped that he would be spared the embarrassment of meeting either Mrs. or Mr. Cline.

Light footsteps sounded beyond the entry, and David straightened.

"Doctor. What a surprise." Josephine looked shocked but greeted him with a warm smile.

"I hope I did not pick an inconvenient time to call. I . . ." *Babbling, I've turned into a babbling fool.*

"I do have another guest. But I insist that you join us."

"Oh, no. I do not wish to intrude. I'll call another time."

"Nonsense."

"I only intended to congratulate you on your idea for the workhouse."

She colored and stepped close. "Thank you. But please, do join us." She whispered, "I'd really like to talk to you."

It was just the encouragement he needed. He felt her gentle touch on his arm and allowed himself to be drawn into a large parlor. To his surprise a young, dark-haired man rose.

"Dr. Wheeler, this is Otis Washburn, reporter for the *Cincinnati Gazette*."

David acknowledged him. "I've read your articles on abolition. Am I interrupting an interview?"

"No," Josephine said.

"Yes. We were . . ." The reporter who spoke at the same time as Josephine drooped under her sharp glance and sank back onto his chair in silence.

David found humor in the way that Josephine took charge of the situation, and like the reporter, David did not have the courage to cross her so he seated himself. The room grew quiet except for Washburn's muffled cough. David clasped his hands together and gazed about the room. Finally, he ventured, "I found today's article about the women's workhouse quite compelling."

"Did you?" both Josephine and Otis Washburn asked simultaneously.

"Why, yes. The idea of a personal patroness is ingenious."

The reporter leaned forward. "Which is exactly what I told Miss Cline the night we attended the benefit ball together."

A burning sensation surged up the back

of David's neck, flushed his face, and settled like a dark cloud across his eyes and temples. There was no way he could conceal his shock and disappointment over Washburn's disclosure that he and Josephine were socially connected.

Josephine frowned and fidgeted with the lace on her bodice. "Now I need to figure a way to attract volunteers. That is why Mr. Washburn is here."

David stood. "I wish you success. But you will not get anything accomplished with me in attendance. I'll call another time."

The reporter stood and offered a handshake. "That is good of you, Doctor."

Josephine stepped forward. "Please, don't go."

"I really have to. I didn't intend to stay."

"At least let me see you to the door."

"No, Miss Cline. That is not necessary."

"Very good of you, Sir. Josephine, I have an idea that might . . ." Washburn's words faded as David made his humiliating departure.

The cold night air slapped his face. What on earth had he been thinking? Josephine did not need his congratulations. She probably had oodles of friends encouraging her, many wishing to be more than friends. In fact, she probably had oodles of suitors with that baby-faced reporter vying to be added to her list.

As he walked, he rehearsed everything he had said and calmed when he realized that he had kept things impersonal. He had done nothing wrong. He only congratulated her on her accomplishments, which were in the area of service that interested him. It had been a socially correct thing to do, nothing more. She would not be able to imagine anything personal. Now he only hoped Josephine would not stir up anything else that involved him. Maybe this would be the end of the story — where he and Josephine were concerned.

Josephine could not get the doctor off her mind. She wondered why he had seemingly changed his mind about cutting off their ties and called upon her the previous night. She reviewed the circumstances of their previous encounters. She had always been the pursuer. At first because she wanted to run him out of town. How long ago that seemed now. Then later to make amends. But after that she had to admit she had just been interested in him. Still he had perceived her intentions and had broken it off between them in the plainest of terms. So why had he come calling? His actions were out of character. Congratulations seemed a flimsy excuse.

He must have changed his mind about her. Her heart raced. Could it be? Or was the issue as simple as he had claimed? If he had changed his mind, why had he left her house in such an abrupt manner? Jealousy or uncertainty over Otis Washburn? Over and over Josephine played the questions through her mind.

A trip to his clinic to apologize for the situation of the night before might be in order. If he was willing to renew their friendship, it might be the nudge he needed. Would that be too forward? Maybe that was the whole problem: He didn't like forward women. He'd said that he didn't like ones with *insulting, unbridled* tongues. She smiled. She couldn't change her personality. With the decision made, she slipped into her cloak and tied the ribbons of her bonnet in place. After leaving a note for her mother, she stepped outside.

Josephine followed the granite paving down the tree-lined causeway of shingle-to-shingle and shoulder-to-shoulder shops and businesses. She paused outside the slate-roofed building with the familiar decorative cornice work and drew in a deep breath, preparing herself to enter. But the door before her magically opened without her assistance.

"Whoa, Josephine!" Dr. Wheeler jerked to a halt outside his clinic and smiled down at her.

His cheerful countenance encouraged her. She returned his smile. "I was hoping to speak with you."

"I'm getting ready to take lunch." He paused momentarily. "Have you had yours?"

"No. Is this an invitation?"

Producing evidence of his bagged lunch, he said, "I'll share mine with you. But I haven't much time."

"I'd like that. Where are we going?"

"Come and you'll see."

She fell into step beside him. They passed storefronts and wood-shuttered windows, but neither broke the silence until they arrived at a plot of vacant land with a stand of oak trees in a secluded area. Squirrels rustled the November-brown grass and crisp leaves.

"What a perfect spot. Do you come here every day?"

"As often as I can get away."

A bird trilled overhead. Otherwise it seemed that they were alone rather than just a stone's throw from the city's hustle and bustle. "I feel like I'm intruding upon what must be the last uncivilized spot in our fair city."

The doctor chuckled as he unwrapped his lunch of smelly cheese and hard bread. "An exaggeration. But it serves as a park. The city board would be smart to buy it up and make it into a real park. But they do not want to do anything that will create a tax. How are we going to ever have a decent city if such measures are not taken?"

"Cincinnati's a place where folks can come and become rich. That's what Father says."

The doctor smirked, then ripped his sandwich in two and offered her half. She peeked between the slices of bread and winced, fearing she would offend him if she did not partake. When he looked up at her again, she swallowed a bite and challenged, "Do not hold in your thoughts on my account."

"But I don't want to ruin our picnic."

"Just tell me."

"I thought that sounded like something your father would say or maybe even something I have already heard him say. I wonder, Josephine, has your father taken over that bright mind of yours entirely? Or is there a section that is still uniquely you, the charming lady?"

"Please do not sugarcoat your words."

"I'm a plain man, simple, straightforward."

"On the contrary, you are a duplicate of your hero, Dr. Daniel Drake."

"Do you know him?"

"Father . . . ," Josephine faltered, then jutting her chin in the air, continued, "Father told me about him and his ideas. He says you are one of his prodigies."

"I would imagine your father has pointed out to you the many differences in our views. It would seem it all only goes to prove one thing. You and I are like oil and water."

She turned her gaze heavenward in disgust. "Ah, yes. Castor oil and lavender water. I remember. I will admit you do irritate me at times. But I also get this glimpse of a good side of you. I'm not willing to disregard our friendship yet. Goodness. If people always had to agree, they wouldn't have many friends, now would they?" She slipped the remainder of her half of the sandwich into her pocket without his noticing.

"Is that why you came to the clinic today?"

"I suppose in part. I wondered why you really came to see me last night. And I also wanted to apologize for your reception. I did not mean for Otis Washburn to frighten you away."

"It sounded like your relationship was more than business."

"It was strictly business."

He struggled. "It was an inopportune time. You have nothing to apologize for. And I only wanted to congratulate you for your efforts at the workhouse. I do admire your caring spirit and your desire to help others."

"I believe that is what I admire about you. That is why I'd like to be friends. Perhaps you can teach me about helping others. Oh, I know what you said. You are a busy man. But surely you can spare me a little time?"

He gazed across the lot, taking time to word his reply. "There are many things that fascinate me. You are one of them. But I need to stay focused on my goals. I fear that a friendship with you would be too distracting."

"I do not understand what is wrong with a little distraction."

"Let me restate my real worry. I fear that knowing you is going to hurt. I'll be torn in two directions; we —"

"You worry an awful lot for such a young man."

"This discussion has been delightful, but speaking of worries reminds me that I need to be getting back to the clinic. I will reconsider your friendship proposal, Josephine."

She stood and straightened her skirt. "I'll say good day then. Thank you for sharing your lunch, Doctor. And for your honesty." She turned and started to walk away.

"Josephine." She paused to look back. He smiled broadly. "You dropped something. And the pleasure has been mine."

It was the sandwich. She shrugged and smiled sheepishly. "I suppose the squirrels are hungrier than I am."

CHAPTER 11

David knocked on Dr. Drake's door and waited. When he was welcomed inside, he followed Drake to the kitchen where the older man poured them each a cup of tea.

"Let's move to the parlor and be comfortable," Drake suggested.

It was an unexpected pleasure to be singled out as a guest in such a home where entertaining groups was commonplace. Drake was a wonderful host, and the conversation was always lively. Many times David had sat in this parlor and listened to a debate or lecture. Tonight he felt honored to be counted among the many friends of Drake's influence, for his acquaintances spread across the nation and came from high positions.

"Put your feet up, my friend." Dr. Drake set his cup down and leaned back in his chair, taking his own advice.

"How is my assistant doing?" David asked.

"He has perseverance, but he is not really ambitious."

"He does not like working at the hospital. He seems better suited to his work at the clinic." He felt guilty for not doing a better job of defending Tom.

"I suppose it is best. How about your cleanup project?"

"I was hoping you would ask. I've an idea I wanted to get your opinion on. I met this reporter, Otis Washburn, who has done a story on a friend of mine. It was about her work at the women's workhouse." Dr. Drake leaned closer, and David continued. "What if I invited a few colleagues and some of the men who sit on the board of health to dig drainage ditches and shovel waste — a workday? I would ask Otis Washburn if he would want to do a story on it to encourage others to participate in our plan."

"Or at the least, they would see your earnest commitment and be more inclined to donate money."

"Exactly."

Drake nodded. "The nation is going through a recession, which isn't helping our organizations that need funding. I'm having trouble getting backing for my hospital, barely breaking even. It does get old begging for money."

"I know the country's finances are tight right now. But Cincinnati's pockets are still bulging."

"Give it a try then. Now drink your tea. Then I'm going to quiz you about this woman friend of yours. I thought you'd been acting differently lately. I sure do miss my Harriet."

David took a couple large gulps of his tea, at first wishing that the other man was not poking into his private life, then realizing he really did need someone to talk to about the woman that both mystified and terrified him. "Josephine Cline's her name. Daughter of Randolph Cline."

Drake's expression turned mysterious as if there were some hidden secret connected with his thoughts, possibly dark, but then he relaxed. "Ah. The bluestocking who brought that scandal down upon your head. Friends, eh?"

"Our relationship would probably better be defined as sparring partners or debating opponents. At first we drew the line, but our paths kept crossing so we've worked at being civil."

"Do you find her attractive?"

David grinned. "Extremely. And I believe the feeling is mutual." He coughed. "She pursued me a bit until I told her I was not interested."

"Why did you do that?"

"We're just too different."

"Nonsense. I hear she's very brilliant. You only need to get her away from that father of hers, and you'll probably find out you have much in common."

"She reveres her father."

"Wait. Back up a bit. What happened when you told her you were not interested?"

"She seemed offended, and we went our separate ways."

"So she's not really your woman friend any longer?"

"After reading the newspaper article about her, I had to see her again so I called on her at her house. That's where I met Otis Washburn. Then she came to my clinic last week to see me."

"Did you treat her kindly?"

"I shared my lunch with her."

"Hah! That would frighten anyone away. But as compassionate a man as you are, I knew there must be some romance in your blood. Do not fight it, my son. I was never happier than when my Harriet was alive. I envy you."

David shrugged. "She proposed friendship. It scares me more than anything I've ever faced."

"Spoken as a true male. What scent does she wear?"

"Lavender."

Drake shook his head and chuckled. "Life will never be the same for you. Might as well pursue her."

"Her father hates me."

Drake's eyes hooded as if he understood. "The perfect challenge."

"That's just it. I'm not sure I can handle all the disruption in my life. I liked it just the way it was." Drake tried to cover a yawn, and David gulped down the rest of his tea. "I didn't mean to bore you with my private life. I really must be going."

"Nonsense. I enjoyed our little talk. Drop in at the hospital again soon."

The *Cincinnati Gazette*'s newspaper office reeked of ink and paper. A man with gartered, rolled-up sleeves glanced at David. "Can I help you?"

"Looking for Otis Washburn."

"You're in luck. Usually he's out and about. But I saw him go into the back room. Have a seat." He nodded toward a bench by the door.

David seated himself, taking in the operation of the printing press, the clamor of wood against paper. He drummed his fingers against the armrest, reassuring himself that this was an important step toward a goal.

Very soon the young, dark-haired reporter entered the rear of the room. Washburn didn't seem to recognize or notice him so David stood and cleared his throat. When Washburn looked, David stepped forward.

"Mr. Washburn." The greeting drew a blank expression. "We met at Josephine Cline's." The dark eyes narrowed. "I've come about a story."

The face reddened. He looked over his shoulder. "Let's sit over there." David followed him to a table. "Is this about Josephine?"

"No. Not at all." The reporter visibly relaxed. "I suppose you've heard the debate over the causes of cholera?"

Washburn leaned forward and plucked a pencil and paper from his pocket. "I'm listening."

As the reporter warmed toward him, David discarded the last trace of animosity he held against the reporter for Josephine's sake and got into the explanation of his story, answering the reporter's questions regarding his theories, or rather Dr. Drake's theories, about cholera being caused by invisible little animal creatures that lived in the filth. "You're not going to make sport of this, are you?" David asked.

The reporter's brow wrinkled. "Let me ask you a question first before I answer that. Are you seeing Josephine?"

"No. But neither are you from what she says."

"Perhaps not at the moment. But I want you to know I am pursuing her. I'm not sure if I should help you."

"Josephine and I are merely friends. I did not have to bring my story to you. I only did so because I thought she was our mutual friend. I could have taken my story to anyone else."

"And I can make a living writing about abolition. Let's leave Josephine out of this for now. I'll give you your story, printing the facts as you give them to me. But I might have to do a follow-up story or two with Dr. Drake about his little imaginary foes."

"Better check your notes. The word was 'invisible.' "

The reporter shook out his paper. "Ah. Yes. Right you are." He grinned, and David wished he had taken his story to a stranger.

"Miss Josephine. You have a caller." The servant gave a perfunctory nod.

"Mr. Washburn. How nice to see you again."

"I came to inquire how the last article worked for you. Did you get volunteers to be personal patronesses to the residents of the workhouse?"

"We did. The program has been implemented. We do not have a patroness for each resident yet, but with time perhaps it can happen. Thank you for your help. You have been too kind."

"Selfishly so, I admit. Actually, I am here on two accounts. I was wondering if I could take you to dinner tonight."

She was afraid that his call might be coming to this. One evening attending a benefit ball with the young man had been enough of his company to suit her. It was never pleasant to let down a young man's hopes. Though the older she got, the less frequently she found herself in such straits.

No excuse presented itself so she opted for the truth. "I hope I have not given you the wrong impression. You are a very fine man, but I only meant our meeting to be about business. If I implied anything else, you have my sincerest apologies."

Washburn reddened and cleared his throat. "You have been quite proper, I assure you. Do not trouble yourself about it any further. But I did enjoy that evening we attended the benefit ball."

"It is best left as a good memory then. And I will think kindly of you when I recall all that you have done to help the women at the workhouse."

"I see."

Washburn chewed on his bottom lip, and Josephine hoped he did not come up with some other angle. How much clearer could she make it? She waited patiently. The room grew very quiet. She wondered if it would be too rude to dismiss either him or herself.

He stood. "Thank you for seeing me. I wish you the best, Miss Cline. And if I can ever be of service again, please consider me able and willing."

"I'll see you to the door."

"No need. I remember the way."

Josephine watched him depart. He was handsome in his smart attire, intelligent, and attentive. She sighed. He had told her that he entertained ambitions of owning his own newspaper one day. His inquiring mind made him an interesting person. They had enjoyed several lively conversations. Unlike many men, he was open-minded when it came to women's opinions and appreciated her curiosity in civic affairs. Most likely he would be successful. She thought wryly that he was everything she should be looking for in a man.

Instead, her thoughts were fixed on a particular eccentric doctor. A man who was not attentive but rather held her off as if she had the plague. A man who could be blunt, rude, and irritating. A man whose ambition was helping the down-and-out and who hoarded his time. Why hadn't David called upon her? She had done everything but offer her friendship on a silver platter. Was the man blind? If she had any sense at all, she would forget about him altogether. But she wasn't ready to do that yet.

Maybe it was time that she had a talk with her mother. Perhaps she could give her advice on how to charm the doctor. Wasn't that what any other female would try? After all, Mother had landed her father, and he was a real catch. Her mother had had several other suitors, too. She knew much more than Josephine about wooing men. It could not be denied that Mother was beautiful, and men always seemed to attend to her. The idea of attracting a man's attention had never enticed Josie. Until now.

CHAPTER 12

Half a dozen shovels hissed into the sludge and splattered muck into vats. David had arranged for the refuse to be loaded onto a flatboat and dumped into the deeper rushing waters of the Ohio River. Next to him an Irishman set the pace. David huffed, finding it hard to keep up with the short man, brawny from hard labor working the canals.

Garbage from the city drained toward the river but collected along Second Street, forming a stinking common sewer. Everyone detested the stench that rose from the area night and day. To eliminate the problem, several men were digging a new drainage ditch so that future rains could wash murky waters all the way into the river.

"Is it true that just breathing in the air might make you sick?" the Irishman asked.

"It's a possibility."

"It's a fear we have. Those who live here."

David hardly knew how to reply. He hoped his efforts would be enough to protect the Irishman and those like him, yet he could not guarantee anything. Only the poorest lived or worked in the area. Although businesses performed their functions along the docks, it was the low-paid laborer who actually performed the work.

Since he had picked up a shovel, he actually felt guilty over the fact that he had been collecting funds to hire the work done — for it was a humiliating and degrading job. Even more amazing, the majority of his volunteers were the poor folks who lived in the area, many of them black. Those he would have hired were doing the work for free.

A splatter of muck struck David in the eyes. He swiped it away with his sleeve. The Irishman laughed.

"Some say that cholera is the result of loose behavior."

"I don't believe that. Cholera originates in places like this. Places where —"

"Us poor folks live."

"Contamination. Stagnant water."

"So you don't think it comes from God?"

"You mean punishment for sins?"

The Irishman nodded.

"I'm no preacher, though my father was,

but the Bible gives many examples where Jesus loves the poor and came to save the sinner. No, I don't think so. If that were the case, I'd probably already be dead."

The Irishman seemed relieved. "I know about God, but I don't always act like it."

Before David could reply, the Irishman's gaze lowered. David looked up to see what had caused the man to withdraw from their conversation. It was Otis Washburn approaching in his fine attire, an expression of distaste on his face.

"This place reeks. How can you stand it?" Otis Washburn grimaced.

David loosened the knot on the handkerchief that covered his mouth. It had been stifling his conversation with the Irishman. "Is that a professional question?"

"Sure it is," Washburn said and grinned.

"The way I see it, the citizens of Cincinnati do not have a choice. This is not a pleasant task. But burying people is even a worse prospect. The lesser of two evils."

"Referring to the possibility of cholera?" David nodded.

"But you're barely making a path through the muck. You're never going to finish. Will you be back tomorrow?"

"Not tomorrow. But next week. I'm hoping that the next time there will be more of us."

"Are these men being paid?"

"No. Everyone is volunteering their time."

"Who are they?"

"Some medical colleagues and students. One is a member of the board of health. Many are residents of the area."

"Residents? How did you get them to help?"

"They do not enjoy living like this. Of course they want to encourage efforts to clean up the place. The next time they'll help recruit volunteers."

"But weren't you seeking funds to pay these people? Looks like they'll do it for free. What will happen to the funds you've collected?"

"I haven't collected any money yet, only pledges. There are people who live in the German part of town, Over the Rhine, who will accept any job."

The whistles from two steamships shrieked, and the reporter's eyes lit. He turned his gaze to the river. "The *Moselle* and the *Goose* are racing again."

David also looked toward the Ohio River. "Someday there's going to be an explosion. They favor speed in lieu of safety when it comes to those big boilers."

127

"Where is your sense of competitiveness? Being the fastest ship is good business. They get the contracts and the glory, too."

"I'm more concerned with sparing lives."

Washburn frowned. "Back to the subject at hand. If you do get it cleaned up, what then? How will you keep it clean?"

"We're digging drainage ditches. Of course when large spring floods come, it will take another community effort to help clean out cellars and low areas where refuse collects. But the drainage ditches should even help with the melting snow in the spring."

"So you've got it all figured out?"

"You mock me. How can I convince you that the support you can solicit through the *Gazette's* story will benefit the citizens of Cincinnati? How can I persuade you to jump on board and help with this worthwhile project?"

"You insult my intelligence."

David leaned on his shovel. "Take care what you publish. You have an obligation to the people of Cincinnati. Do not take such a responsibility lightly."

"That sounds a lot like a threat."

"Only the truth."

"Truth is something each person must find for themselves."

"I don't agree. It's always the same

whether people find it or not."

Washburn chuckled. "One thing I know for truth: When you finish here, you'll need to take a long bath. I believe I have enough for my story." He tipped his hat. "Doctor."

David watched the reporter leave. He repositioned the handkerchief over his mouth and returned to his shoveling. As he worked, he wondered how he managed of late to defeat his own good purposes. He only hoped that he didn't end up in another scandal of some sort. The earth opened as his tool sliced in. The smart-mouthed reporter was right about one thing: A long hot bath was more than called for.

"Mother. Can you spare some time for me?"

Mrs. Cline turned away from her sewing project. "I'm always happy to chat with you, Dear. I just didn't hear you enter the room."

Josie lounged in one of the plush parlor chairs beside her mother. "I need some advice."

Mrs. Cline's face lit with pleasure. "Oh? I'll be delighted to help if I can."

A sudden rush of heat warmed Josie's neck. "I've never given much thought to attracting men, but now I've met someone, and I'm wondering how to catch his interest."

Her mother could not disguise her surprise though she kept her voice level. "My, my. You wish to charm a gentleman?" She struggled to compose her enthusiasm. "It might help if I knew who he was."

"I guess I was hoping for some sure remedy that would work on all men. But I don't suppose all men are equal." She shrugged and stood. "Never mind. Nothing may even come of this anyway."

"Nonsense! You are most charming." Mrs. Cline studied her daughter. "I do not mean to brag, but I've never had a problem with men. I will help you. Now tell me everything."

Josie sank back into the chair and sighed. "It's Dr. Wheeler." Her mother's eyes widened, resembling the teacups stacked in the cabinet on the wall behind her. "You are disappointed. He is the most interesting man I've ever met. He's quite compassionate. And you have seen for yourself that he is extremely handsome."

"How well I remember his passion and the uproar he caused at the fundraiser dinner."

"He had every reason to be angry. I falsely accused him."

"Hmm. From what I gleaned watching him at the workhouse, his type is probably sincere, serious. If he's a doctor, he's probably very studious and devoted to his work."

Josie was pleased and amazed at her mother's understanding. "You have accurately described him. I think he is attracted to me, but he's very jealous of his time and thinks a friendship with me will infringe upon his career."

Her mother looked aghast. "All of this has already been discussed?"

"I'm not shy, Mother."

"No. Of course not. If it is the doctor who you want to attract, then I will help you. And if nothing comes from it, at least the practice will be good for you."

"Mother!"

Mrs. Cline was not chagrined and delved into the perplexity with all earnestness. "Let's see. I think we need to appeal to his sense of reasoning, make loving you seem the most logical conclusion in the world."

"Love? I only want to be his friend."

"Really? Whoever heard of such a thing?" She rattled on before Josie could form a sound argument. "We can start there, I suppose. Make a list of the things that your love
—"

"Friendship."

"Friendship would offer. Then go down the list one by one until you have made each point evident to him. Think about areas of his life that knowing you would enhance. Then when you have thought about how you will apply yourself, plan a strategy that will demonstrate explicitly."

Josie frowned. "I do not want to trick him or coerce him into anything. I was just looking for some simple ways to attract his attention."

"I didn't mean to make things sound complicated. It's just a matter of applying your charm."

"I suppose. It's all new to me. Thank you, Mother. I think I'll go work on my list."

"What list?"

Josie jumped at the sound of her father's voice.

"Ingredients of a recipe. One that has been handed down among the women of the family," Mrs. Cline said, a glint in her eyes.

"Oh." Randolph Cline sat down with his newspaper. "You'll never guess, Josie, what your scandalous Dr. Spokes is up to."

Josie and Mrs. Cline instantly gave him their attention. Josie tried to sound nonchalant. "I haven't heard any rumors."

"Otis Washburn, your reporter, came to see me today."

"Father, he's not my doctor and definitely

132

not my reporter."

"He told me that Spokes was shoveling manure down at the docks. Remember when he asked for my help in cleaning up the city? Well he must not have gotten much response because he's down there doing the work himself." He chuckled. "If I didn't dislike the man so, I'd credit him for his grit. He apparently hopes to drum up some excitement over the project by giving the story to your reporter."

She ignored her father's teasing. "Why did Mr. Washburn tell you about it?"

"He found out somehow that I'd turned down the doctor. Washburn wanted to interview someone with an opposing opinion on the issue. I don't believe he thinks much of your doctor either."

A lump formed in Josie's stomach. Her father was forming an even bigger wall between her and David. "Is the article in there?"

"No. It will be in tomorrow's paper."

"I'll be sure to read it. I think I'll go to my room now. I've some things to attend to. Good night."

Josie cast her mother a beseeching glance, then hurried to her room and closed the door behind her, throwing herself across her bed to think. This could not turn out well. Whatever her father had said, it was bound to make David angry. And it was all her fault. She should have told her father how much she liked David from the beginning. Perhaps then he would have defended David for her sake. Her father loved her and would do anything for her. But now David's anger over this new incident was sure to spill over to include her. And to think that only minutes ago making a list was her biggest concern.

It occurred to her that maybe Otis Washburn was doing this because he was jealous of David. And if that were the case, David would have even more reason to blame her. There was nothing to be done about any of it until she had read the article. If she thought it would do any good, she would go to the *Gazette*'s office. But of course it wouldn't, for the story was probably already going to print.

CHAPTER 13

David hurriedly sliced some bread and cheese and poured himself a steaming cup of coffee. He could hardly contain his curiosity over the morning's paper. With a snap of his wrists, it fell open, and he scanned the headlines for the article. LOCAL DOCTOR PRONOUNCES WAR AGAINST INVISIBLE ARMY. David groaned as he read:

Grimy from head to toe and reeking, Dr. David Wheeler led a band of doctor colleagues and medical students as well as a few local residents in what he proclaims to be a citywide cleanup campaign. Although his reasoning seems a bit absurd — rounding up the invisible animal creatures that cause cholera and other disease and disposing of them into the muddy waters of the Ohio River — no one is complaining about his efforts.

Sensible citizens realize that the stench from Second Street is a detriment to health. So although the doctor's reasoning may be debatable, the results are favorable.

He hopes to bring the need to the attention of Cincinnati's prominent citizens. You may show your support by donating funds. The money will pay immigrants to perform the required labor. Dr. Wheeler was encouraged when many local residents also pitched in to help, eager to see the sludge and slime removed from their neighborhood.

The question remains: Will his efforts be worthwhile? Will they make a difference? Dr. Wheeler's response to this question was that new drainage ditches to the river are being planned and another workday is scheduled for Saturday of next week. He invites anyone who has some spare time to come with shovels and join in the adventure.

In order to get a feel for the response of the public, I interviewed Mr. Randolph Cline, land developer and textile factory owner.

David's pulse increased. What sort of trick

was this? Hadn't Washburn poked enough fun already?

It seems that the good doctor has made his rounds, for Randolph Cline was already familiar with the campaign. The doctor had confronted him about a month earlier to beg funds. From the mouth of Randolph Cline: "The plan is foolhardy because it wastes money on something frivolous. The nation is presently in an economic panic. It is already a tight year financially. There are plenty of real problems for Cincinnati's citizens to consider. Issues pertaining to shipping and land development. Pursuits that enrich our city, not just beautify it."

Randolph Cline also felt personally belittled when the doctor used threatening tactics, indicating that Cline's family could be the next to die of cholera. I also asked Mr. Cline what he thought about the local residents who showed up to volunteer. "That is how it should be. Everyone should sweep their own stoop, clean their own property. Then we wouldn't have this problem. Why should I pay to clean up someone else's dirt or worse? Anyway, it is a well-known fact that Dr. Wheeler is an eccentric."

I would be remiss if I did not present the

question to you, the citizen. Is Cincinnati clean enough? If not, will you join forces with Dr. David Wheeler and do something to help? Mr. Clay Buchanan of the Cincinnati Hardware Store says that he will furnish free shovels to anyone wishing to get involved. This should come as no surprise as Buchanan is a member of the board of health.

David shook his head. Washburn treated it all as a big joke. He felt discouraged over the results he would get from such an article as this. One thing for sure, next week he wouldn't ask Washburn to cover the story. And as for Randolph Cline, he was fast becoming an opponent if not an enemy. He supposed that would put an end to any dreams of pursuing a friendship with his beautiful daughter.

Josephine read her father's newspaper and shuddered. It was a far cry from the kind of support and coverage Otis had given her regarding her idea of a personal patroness for each woman at the workhouse. As for her father, she was disappointed with him for the first time in her life. Of course he had no idea of her feelings for the doctor. It was not like he was deliberately hurting her.

But just reading the article and imagining how David might be feeling about it caused her to view her father's opinions under a new light. He had sounded cold, money-hungry, uncaring. She had never crossed purposes with Father before and feared the results of such a course, not wanting to hurt him.

Would there be any hope now for her and David? Perhaps it was foolish to wish that David and her father might accept each other. David might even refuse to see her again. Several times he had implied that she blindly followed after her father's view-points. If she went to him and told him that she did not agree with her father on this is-sue, it might open a door toward a relation-ship. Then if her father would reconsider his stand when he saw how much it meant to her and give David a chance . . .

Spurring herself on with such hopeful thinking, she took out the list she had been compiling, considering the first point: *David and I are both interested in the well-being of others, especially the downtrodden.*

Keeping in line with her mother's sugges-tions, now she needed to plan an event to demonstrate this point. She chewed on her pencil pensively. Suddenly, the solution was obvious. One that would win his heart if nothing else could. By this one action she would not even have to say a word about the newspaper article — except perhaps to explain to her father afterward. He would be livid when word got to him that his own daughter had showed up at the doctor's next workday, shovel in hand. To be sure, it would cause a scandal. But as long as the doctor appreciated her efforts, she didn't care what the rest of the world thought.

That afternoon David looked up to see Tom Langdon poke his plump head through a gap in the clinic's curtains. "A Mr. Bartholomew Hastings to speak with you." David had approached the man weeks ago about the cleanup campaign, but he had refused to donate any funds. David had attributed it to the benefit dinner scandal. He wondered now if Hastings had changed his mind.

"Mr. Hastings. What can I do to help you?"

Hastings thrust his hand inside his vest and withdrew a pouch. "I'd like to make a contribution to your cause. I'm not sure about your tiny invisible animal theory." He chuckled. "But I like your determination. You've won me over, Doctor."

"Thank you for your generosity. The citizens of Cincinnati thank you. I'll take this to the bank right away. I believe I mentioned before that I have set up a fund which will be supervised by the board of health."

"Yes. I imagine you'll be working with them a lot in these coming days." He grinned as if he were privy to some great secret.

"I hope so. Be sure to pass the word."

He chuckled again. "Oh, word is spreading. I'll run along now. We're both busy men."

"Thank you again."

Once the man had disappeared, David let out a whoop and pumped his arm in the air. After that, his imaginings of crossing another name off his list were interrupted as the bell on the clinic's door jingled again.

"Congratulations, Doctor."

This time it was Clay Buchanan. David smiled. "I guess you've read the paper, too."

"Indeed I have. And I overheard your jubilance after Hastings' departure. But the fact is, the board met this morning. We've decided to bring you aboard, Doctor. Your methods may be unconventional, but we think you're just what we need. What Cincinnati needs. Will you accept the position?"

"I'm honored. How can I refuse?"

"Wonderful!" Clay patted David's shoulder. "We'll call a meeting to indoctrinate you and help organize your next workday."

With the assistance that David received after that from the board of health, everything escalated so fast that by the morning of the next workday fifty people had gathered, many with shiny new shovels donated by Clay Buchanan's store. Many had returned, such as the Irishman, and David recognized several of his former patients.

The board helped to instruct the volunteers. An engineer, whom David had recruited the previous week, supervised the digging of new drainage ditches. David had finished organizing this group when he felt a light tap upon his shoulder. He turned.

"Josephine?" His mouth fell agape. "What are you doing here?"

She lifted her shiny new shovel and pointed toward Clay and some of the other board members. "They insisted that I report directly to you."

He pointed at the shovel in her grip. "Surely you do not intend to use that?" The skirt of her pretty wool dress was already soiled beyond repair. "The job is strenuous and foul."

"I'm strong. I can work for awhile."

David warmed at her enthusiasm. "Really, Josephine, I do appreciate the gesture. But I am sure there is something more suitable that you can do to help. We could use some refreshments. I know it is short notice, but if you could organize some women —"

She surrendered her shovel to him. "I'll do it."

Again he felt astonished. "Great!" Relief and an overwhelming gratitude for her cooperation rushed in.

She flashed him a smile and started to go. He had to squelch the urge to hug her. "Josephine."

She turned.

"Thank you."

"Just doing my civic duty, Doctor." She smiled again and left.

He leaned against the shovel she had abandoned. Joy curled up inside him.

True to her word, an hour later she returned with several other women and continued to be a bright spot in the mire and ooze.

Another incident occurred, however, that was not so favorable. "Doctor! Come quick!" David wheeled about. "We found a black man, half dead!"

Abandoning his shovel, David hurried after the messenger to the circle of men who had gathered around the victim. He barely breathed. "Let's get him to the hospital."

"It's the bad air. We're all going to die," someone said. Several shovels fell discarded. Men fled. Others hesitated, as did David, for he did not know whether to go along to the hospital or stay and reassure the volunteers. The matter was decided when his assistant, Tom, suddenly appeared.

"Want me to take him to the clinic?"

"No. To the hospital so I can stay here and try to keep everyone calm." Thankfully David left the patient in Tom's care and turned to reason with the group of disgruntled men. "That man had nothing to do with what's going on here. He wasn't one of our volunteers."

"What's wrong with him?"

"I don't know."

"Then you don't know for sure he didn't get sick from the rotten air."

One of the board members drew David aside. "Perhaps we should call it a day."

"You're right." He turned back to the agitated group. "Everyone go home. Better to be safe. And thank you for your participation. Cincinnati thanks you!"

The men began to disassemble, murmuring. David felt exhausted, bone weary.

"David?" a female voice asked. "What happened?"

"Oh, Josephine." David backed away from

her. "I'm so dirty."

She smiled and shrugged. "I don't care. I'm not afraid."

"You're very brave. Thank you for helping. We're quitting for today."

"I'd better get Mother then and —"

"Your mother came?" David asked, incredulous.

Josephine chuckled. "I didn't want to face Father's wrath alone."

Once again David felt the urge to hug her. But, of course, that was impossible. "Will you go to dinner with me tomorrow night?" He blushed. "I hope the stench will be gone by then."

"I'd love to meet you for dinner."

For the moment, he cast Randolph Cline's likely reaction from his mind. "The Emerald Inn at seven o'clock."

Josephine nodded, picked up her ruined skirts, and tromped off. In David's eyes she was every bit the lady.

He stood there watching her departure. Somewhere behind him he heard evidence that the *Moselle* was racing again. Around him clouds of smoke drifted over the city's steam foundries. Beyond, Cincinnati's green hills looked hazy and indistinct.

Josephine and her mother giggled together

145

as they soaked in tubs of hot water and suds. "That was the most outrageous thing I've ever done in my life," Mrs. Cline admitted.

"And it was only number one on my list," Josephine said as she gave an impish grin.

Mrs. Cline groaned. "What have I done? I'm afraid to ask, but what is number two?"

"He's a terrible cook."

"And you're an excellent one." Mrs. Cline wrinkled her brow. "How do you know he's a bad cook?"

Josephine blushed.

CHAPTER 14

"You are not going out!" Randolph Cline thundered. "I wish to speak with you."

Josephine bristled at the unusually harsh tone and bossy command. "Father, I am not a child. I am twenty-two years old."

His eyes narrowed. "With yesterday's stunt it appears you are about five years old." His words hurt, and he must have sensed it for he added in a softer tone. "What are you up to now? It's late to be going out."

"I'm meeting a friend for dinner at the Emerald Inn."

He calmed even more and appealed to her in earnest. "Come sit beside me, Josephine. This is all so unlike you."

Of course she had known this discussion was due, only the timing was horrid. She perched on the edge of the couch. "All right, Father. But I am in a hurry."

He ran a hand through his neatly combed

hair. "I cannot understand why you and your mother joined this cleanup crusade. Surely you understood that I was opposed to it? After that article in the *Gazette*, this looks bad for me, Josie. If I cannot handle my own household, others will think I am weak. It puts my business in jeopardy."

"Handle your household? Do you mean to infer that we are your puppets? I am shocked, Father. I always thought you encouraged me to use my brain. And now for the first time that I have a different opinion, you mean to squelch it."

"You have always thought and acted wisely before."

"Just because I agreed with you?"

His facial muscles tightened. "I am your father. I have authority over you and your mother."

"Isn't that a bit harsh?" Mrs. Cline interjected as she entered the room. "You've always encouraged our charitable pursuits, Randolph."

Josie patted his knee. "And if it is any consolation, I did not do anything to intentionally make you look foolish. I only did this because it is something that I personally believe in."

He narrowed his eyes. "Why have you changed your mind about Dr. Spokes?"

148

After giving her father a dirty look for ridiculing David's name again, Josie said, "It is simple. I was wrong about him. He's a very nice, sweet man."

"Nice? Sweet?" Randolph's mouth twisted with distaste.

"I believe this can all be settled by inviting the doctor to dinner," Mrs. Cline suggested.

Josie and her father both stared at Mrs. Cline as if she had grown two heads. Josephine recovered first for upon giving it a little thought, it wasn't such a bad idea. In fact, it fit in quite nicely with number two on her list.

"I'm sorry we upset you, Father. But I must hurry before I miss my friend. Can we talk about this later?"

"Who are you meeting?" he asked again.

Josie scooted off the sofa and gave her father a kiss on the cheek. "Just a very lovely friend. Thank you for worrying over us. Why don't you and Mother plan a date for inviting the doctor over?" She eased away and started toward the door. Behind her she heard her father's mutter.

"I didn't agree to any such dinner."

"Nonsense, Darling . . ."

Josie smiled. She knew her mother could charm away her father's objections. Her appreciation of her mother's feminine abilities was increasing. Now if she hurried, she would not be too late for her date.

David smelled the lovely lavender scent and looked up in anticipation.

"Forgive me for being late. I hoped you would not give up on me."

"I was worried. I do not like your coming unescorted. We're going to have to do something about our meeting like this. We must be open with your father."

"I agree. When I left the house, Mother and Father were planning a date to invite you to dinner. That's why I'm late."

"What?"

"I don't mean to be forward. You did say we're going to have to do something about meeting like this."

"But your father wants me to come to dinner?" He narrowed his eyes. "Is this some kind of trap?"

She frowned. "You're getting dangerously close to being rude."

Josephine was right. He had responded badly. "Forgive me. Let's order, then we'll start again. I promise to be a gentleman."

"Agreed."

Josephine gave her order to the waiter. Her face was still flushed from the outdoors. The radiance of her face captivated David. Once the waiter had gone, he told her so. "Miss Cline, you look lovely this evening. And I mean that with all sincerity. The only thing that could compare is the loveliness of your heart." He chuckled and shook his head. "I still cannot believe that you showed up with a shovel."

Her eyes lit. "Which reminds me that I hear congratulations are in order. You have been elected to the board of health. Surely this will help to serve your purposes."

"It already has. Do you know that I got the whole idea from watching you?"

"I do not understand."

"The way you helped out at the workhouse — doing something out of the ordinary — made me consider my situation and how I could apply myself."

Josephine giggled, covering her mouth.

"What's so funny?"

"Why, you were my inspiration. The way you go to the slums canvassing patients. Your example provoked my actions at the workhouse."

David leaned close, propping his chin in the cup of his hand, his elbow resting on the table. "Do you suppose we complement each other? Surely we cannot be bringing out the best in each other? I mean, all this time I thought we were like —"

"Two explosive elements." She shook her head. "Surely not. It must be an isolated case. I'm sure we'll be back to bickering before this dinner is over."

"Not if you keep behaving in such a captivating manner."

She shoved her hand toward him across the table. "Could it mean that we are friends at last?"

He clasped it tightly. "Yes, Josephine, I suppose it does. *O dofo ho ye ha*."

"What does that mean?"

"African. A good friend is hard to come by."

"It's beautiful. Thank you. Does this mean that you will come to dinner then?"

David withdrew his hand and closed his eyes. When he opened them, she was dabbing at her eyes. They were teary. "If they invite me, I will come." He smiled. "But I am curious — who will be cooking this dinner? Servants? Your mother or you?"

She giggled. "Probably a combination of all three of us."

"I shall look forward to it."

Their food came, and for awhile they turned their attention to it. Josie felt a little guilty over his comment about their complementing each other in their efforts of benevolence. It seemed eerily close to her own wording of point number one on her list. And number two was on its way to being implemented. Since things were going so well, perhaps she should move right along to point number three on her list — encouraging each other in their faith in Christ.

"You mentioned that your parents were missionaries in Africa. Tell me about your family." His expression instantly revealed a love for his family.

"My mother died when I was born. But Claire, the woman I call my mother, cared for me from the beginning. My father was a preacher. When I was a baby, he was framed for murder. For awhile he and Claire took me and hid from the law. In the end, he was acquitted. By this time he had fallen in love with Claire. They married and returned to Father's church. But only for a short time. Then they took me to West Africa with them while they served as missionaries. As it turned out, Claire and Father never had any other children."

"That is quite a story. What an intriguing past. No wonder you are an extraordinary man."

He shrugged.

"Are your folks still living?"

"Yes. But they are presently abroad."

"They must miss you. How long have you lived in the United States?"

"They came home while I was a teen. I stayed in Beaver Creek, Ohio, with relatives when they returned."

"Oh? What relatives?"

"I have a whole gang of them. I call them the Tucker House bunch."

"How is it that you came to Cincinnati?"

"I heard about Dr. Drake." His tone was reprimanding as if she should have known.

"Of course," she said, feeling an aversion toward this Dr. Drake who had such a hold on David. She had only met Drake once or twice.

"When did you come to Cincinnati?" he asked.

"I was born here."

The waiter interrupted with a question about dessert, but they both declined.

"I should be getting home before dark."

"I'll hail a hackney and take you home."

"That isn't necessary."

"But it is. Come."

David found a hackney and assisted her into it. He was so considerate. Her thoughts rambled. "What happened to the man you found half dead?"

"He survived, but he's very weak. It's a

shame. He has no home. He's not a slave, but he cannot find work. Always on the move."

"I'm sorry." They both grew reflective. Eventually Josephine asked, "Do you think this will stop the volunteers?"

"I don't know. People have erroneous ideas about cholera. Some still believe it's a moral issue and cholera comes from the poor and immoral." He scowled. "Ridiculous idea."

"I'm proud of you. The work you're doing."

"That means a lot to me."

They rode in silence after that, but it was a comfortable quiet. She realized that although they skirted around the subject, they hadn't actually talked about their faith in God. She would bring it up the next time she saw him. She felt assured that there would be another time. He'd promised to come to dinner, and he'd said those beautiful words about friendship.

The carriage jerked to a stop. David stepped down and then helped her descend. He continued to hold her hand.

"Thank you for a lovely dinner," she said.

"I'll look forward to our next one," he replied.

Josie walked to her front door and turned

back. David still stood outside the hackney's open door. He waved. She waved back and went inside, her heart happily skipping.

CHAPTER 15

"I'm going to lunch. Go ahead, Tom, and take care of our next patient." Outside the clinic, David inhaled the crisp November air and felt happy. In the past week there had been another workday. And he hadn't even had to be there. Some of the other board of health members had taken charge. David had been overloaded at the clinic with winter sicknesses. The event had been successful. Even Zachary Caulfield, the last person on his list, had come over to the cause and donated money. This was after Mrs. Caulfield helped Josie and Mrs. Cline with refreshments for the workers.

All in all, his project had been successful. And now with winter's approach he felt confident that the cholera would be suppressed. Of course in the spring the campaign would need to be taken up again.

As he walked, his thoughts turned to Josephine, and he wondered why he had not heard any more about the proposed dinner invitation. Perhaps there had been a disagreement at her household when the intended dinner had been discussed. Maybe he should call on her. But he didn't want to get her into trouble. He chuckled. She wasn't bashful. She would show up at the clinic one of these days. Heaven knew he had enough to keep him busy in the meantime. Of late his clinic overflowed to the point that he sent many of their patients directly to the hospital.

He rounded a corner and noticed some boys dicing. "Shall I call the authorities?" David asked with sternness.

Instantly, they scattered. When he looked up at the pathway again, the object of his thoughts stood before him, bundled in a winter cloak and muff. She waved. Her cheeks were flushed from the cold. Some errant hair framed her smiling face. His steps quickened toward her.

"Hello. I didn't know if you still came here since the weather's gotten so cold."

"Today is the first time I've been able to get away all week. The clinic is so busy right now."

"I've been busy also. With the cold turn, we've admitted more women to the workhouse. I'm sorry I couldn't make your workday. But I did make arrangements for some other women to take my place."

"Don't be sorry. I didn't make it either. All your efforts are appreciated."

"Did it go well?"

"Yes. Each time we get more volunteers and more exposure."

"Speaking of exposure, it probably wasn't the wisest idea to employ Mr. Washburn to cover your story."

"So I discovered. I believe he was jealous over you."

Josephine colored. "Probably. But I certainly haven't encouraged him. Would you like me to have a talk with him?"

"No. Don't worry about it. Let's sit. You want to share my lunch?"

"What do you have?"

"A sandwich."

"I'll just watch you eat."

"So what brings you here?"

"I've come to extend that dinner invitation we discussed earlier."

David smiled. "You actually procured one? Does your father know?"

"Yes. And he's promised me to be open-minded. And you must promise me the same."

"Of course. When?"

"Friday evening. Now I've got to go."

"Thank you, Josephine. I'll be praying about this dinner."

She gave him an enormous smile. "Me, too. Bye, then."

David watched her leave. The scent of lavender in early winter was a strangely wonderful thing.

Friday evening arrived. David's step was lively. His heart already beat madly. He rounded the corner two blocks from the Clines'. Once again, it troubled him to see a group of young lads playing dice. They recognized him and rose to scatter before he said a word. But as the lads made to disperse, he noticed a familiar face. "Master Schroeder! Wait!"

The boy stiffened, turned slowly. He looked instantly remorseful. David hurried to the lad. "Since when have you taken to the dice? Surely you know that is a perfect way to squander your money. And it is illegal."

"Some money I saved. Not enough. To make it grow, I wanted."

"Is your mother ill?"

"She's *gut,* but gone is Papa's money. In the streets she'll be."

"I'm sorry. But if it should come to that, I hear the women's workhouse is not such a

160

bad place. Your employer, Randolph Cline — his wife and daughter work there."

"She'll not go there. To die she would first go. A job she had until another curse the neighbor did. She lost it then."

The superstition again. Remorseful that he had not followed up on presenting the gospel to the woman as he had earlier planned, David grasped at the opportunity to get involved again. "I'll make you a deal. You quit dicing, and I'll go visit your mother and see what I can do to help her."

The lad nodded. *"Danke."*

David hoped Mrs. Cline would have an idea of a job for Mrs. Schroeder. He would speak to her tonight if the opportunity presented itself.

He knocked. The familiar servant invited him in, seated him, and withdrew to find Josephine.

"David." Josephine swept into the room dressed in a pale green silk gown. "I'm so happy to see you." She moved close and whispered, "You look very fine. Let me take you to meet Mother and Father." She drew him down the hallway and just before they entered an adjoining room released his hand and gave an encouraging smile. "Ready?"

He nodded though he dreaded the encounter as much as the plague. They entered the room. Randolph Cline was reading, and Mrs. Cline sat beside him. Both of them looked up. Josephine said, "Our guest has arrived. May we join you?"

"Please do." Mrs. Cline agreed with a smile.

Randolph set his reading material aside. He leaned back, twiddled his thumbs, and quietly studied David.

"Thank you," David said. "It was kind of you to invite me."

The room grew awkwardly quiet, and David remained standing. "Sit down, Doctor. Seems the women cooked up more than dinner this evening. We might as well make the best of a bad situation."

"Father!"

"Randolph!"

"Quite so, Sir," David said, seating himself.

Once again the room grew oppressively quiet. "You've a lovely home."

"I've worked hard for it," Cline growled. "Don't squander my money."

David glanced at Josephine. She was biting her lower lip; her pretty brow was furrowed. Much to David's relief; a servant appeared and announced dinner. David was seated across from Randolph between Mrs. Cline and Josephine. They waited as the servants brought various dishes.

"You set a lovely table, Mrs. Cline."

"The cloth was my mother's."

"An heirloom?"

"Why, yes."

"Lovely," he said again for want of something more intelligent to say. Then he remembered something that might be of interest to his hostesses. "Oh. I brought you ladies something. The name of a woman who would like to be one of your personal patronesses."

He reached into his vest pocket, and when he withdrew his hand, several dice rolled out onto the table. When they tumbled, he quickly made a mad grab for them realizing how bad such a thing must look. As he did, he knocked over Josephine's glass, and dark juice splattered making a giant stain on Mrs. Cline's beautiful heirloom tablecloth.

She gasped. Both hands covered her mouth.

Randolph quickly leaped up to avoid getting a lapful of liquid. From his lofty position he glared down at David.

"I am so sorry. I apologize." David frantically grabbed at things until Josie grabbed his sleeve.

"Stop. It's all right. Please, stop."

David nodded and rose. He stood back so

the servants could clean up the mess.

After what seemed like an eternity, Mr. Cline sat back down, mumbling something about *still causing a ruckus.*

The atmosphere at the table grew painfully quiet. Josephine took up the paper with the woman's name and slipped it into her bodice.

"Let me explain about the dice. I broke up a group of lads playing on the street."

Randolph Cline raised a disbelieving brow.

"In fact, you would know one of the lads," David said. "That Schroeder boy. Isn't he your apprentice?"

Randolph scowled. "He was gambling?"

"Yes, but he gave me his dice. In return I am supposed to call upon his mother and see if I can find her a job. I thought maybe you could help, Mrs. Cline. I intended to ask you about it."

"Well, of course, she can come to the workhouse, and we'll see what we can do."

"The boy doesn't seem to think she would come. She doesn't like charity."

"That's sad. I don't know what we can do if she will not accept our help."

The room grew quiet.

"Taste your food, David," Josephine said.

David took a bite and was wondrously pleased. "This is so delicious."

"Josephine made it," Mrs. Cline said.

"I had no idea you could cook like this. That's the bad part about being a bachelor. My cooking is so terrible my cat won't even eat it."

Josephine blushed.

"Maybe you should hire Mrs. Schroeder to do your cooking," Mr. Cline suggested. His eyes held a shrewd glint of satisfaction.

"That's a wonderful idea," Mrs. Cline agreed. "What do you think, David?"

"I could use some help." David thought about how he wanted the opportunity to speak with Mrs. Schroeder about the Lord. "Yes. I believe she just might do it. I'll ask."

The rest of the meal passed uneventfully in comparison to its beginning. But when they rose from the table, Randolph Cline asked David, "May I talk with you privately?" Josephine looked as if she wanted to intervene on David's behalf but wasn't sure how to accomplish it, so he had no choice but to follow Randolph into his study.

"Josie always was one to bring home strays."

David did not want to play games. "It seemed like you and I got on well enough until I mentioned Dr. Drake's name. What is it between you two?"

The point had hit its mark. "A private matter. Nothing that concerns you." He eased down into his chair.

"Did you want to speak about Josephine, or do you wish for me to diagnose your malady? Is it back pain?"

Randolph scowled again and disregarded the latter part of the question. "What are your intentions regarding my daughter?"

"We would like to be friends."

"You're not intent upon courting her?"

David choked and coughed. "Excuse me?"

"You're a doctor. You know about men and women, courting, marriage, babies."

"Please. I would describe our relationship along the lines of sparring partners. We click intellectually."

Cline's face softened. "My Josie is very bright. That's why it puzzles me that she brought you home."

"I'm an honorable man. I can give you credentials if that's what it takes to be allowed to have a friendship with Josephine."

"I've already checked your credentials. A long time ago. The only thing that comes up short is your eccentricity and your connection to Drake. I'm willing to give you a try. But just remember that I'll be watching you. Don't slip up."

"I'll remember. Now let's talk about your

hemorrhoids."

Randolph's mouth gaped open. "How did you know? That daughter of mine —"

"Didn't say a word. I can tell by your actions. Let me get my black bag. I've got some turpentine and castor oil in there that will make a new man out of you. And if that doesn't work, we'll try some salt in buffalo tallow."

"Humph!"

CHAPTER 16

"David. Come in. Sit down." He did so, wondering why Dr. Drake had called this special meeting. "I'm very pleased with the outcome of your cleanup campaign."

Efforts had been switched from actual cleaning up of debris to digging drainage ditches. The weather would soon turn the ground frigid, and once it snowed, the debris would not be a problem until spring. The drainage ditches would accommodate spring floods and snow runoff. Most of the funds collected had been put into hiring engineers and labor for the digging. Each morning after David made his trek along the docks or the canal, he would swing by various sites and speak encouragement to the workers.

"I'm happy enough with the results. Of course I'll take the matter up again in the spring."

"Your appointment on the board of health

will remind you of keeping to your goals, I am sure. But I am so pleased with your work that I've an offer to make you. I want you to become my personal assistant."

Panic struck David. Winter was around the corner. Sickness had already snowballed. He didn't have time for anything new. "What did you have in mind?"

"Frankly I could use some help soliciting funds for the hospital."

David detested soliciting. Above all things, he did not wish to acquire another fund-raising project. "I'm very busy. The clinic is overflowing. I'm afraid I shall have to decline for now."

"You could give the clinic to your assistant to run."

Releasing a large sigh, David shrugged. "Honestly I don't see how."

"Come work with me at the hospital. Travel with me. Help me with my writing. All my projects." Drake chuckled. "I can see that I've overwhelmed you. Take some time. Give it some thought. But remember. I need you."

Give it some thought, David repeated Dr. Drake's words as he stepped out into the street. The sky looked menacing. He pulled his cloak tight around his neck and tried to take in the propensity of Drake's offer. It was the compliment of a lifetime to be asked to be his personal assistant. Quite the achievement. He never would have dreamed that Drake would even consider it. But even more amazing was that he didn't want to do it. He didn't feel like he could find contentment in shifting from one thing to another like Drake did. And now with his budding friendship with Josephine, it didn't seem prudent to take on more work. The obvious deterrent was how this position with Drake would push her father over the edge.

On the other hand, how could he dismiss such an honor to work with the greatest physician he had ever met? He couldn't do it lightly.

He glanced upward again and sniffed the air. Their first snow might arrive this very day. By the time he had reached this point in his thoughts, he had also arrived at Mrs. Schroeder's apartment. He knocked on her door.

"Doctor. Come in."

The living quarters were cold and somehow bleaker. "How is your health?" David asked. It was hard to tell if the woman was thinner with all the layers of clothes she wore.

She spoke in her native language. "Fine,

thanks to your potion. But that old hen next door hasn't gotten any easier to live around."

"I'm sorry to hear that."

"What can I do for you?" she asked.

"I was hoping that you could help me out with a problem. You see, I live alone, and I'm a terrible cook. You wouldn't know anyone who I could hire to help me out?"

Her eyes brightened. "Do you like German food?"

"I do. Believe me, I'd be grateful for anything that I didn't have to cook."

"How much would you be willing to pay? I don't mean to sound negative, but by the looks of your suit, you don't have much money to spare."

He mentioned a tidy sum.

Her eyes looked disbelieving. "You sure you can afford that?"

"You have my word."

"I believe I'd like to apply for the job myself."

"Hired! When can you start?"

"Today."

"Excellent. Here's some money for supplies. I live across the canal at Vine and Eighth Streets."

"Really? I would have guessed you lived down at the docks or —"

"I live behind my clinic."

"My, my. You are full of surprises today."

"My kitchen is very small. Make yourself at home there. I never know for sure when I'll be home. But I want you to leave before it gets dark. You can just set aside my supper for me."

"But what about washing the dishes?"

"I can wash dishes. I just can't cook."

"Or you can leave them for me for the next day."

"We can work out the details as we go."

"Thank you. I really need a job. I believe fate has been good to me and that curse has been reversed for good." She cackled. "If only the old hen knew."

"I'd rather believe that God has brought us together."

Mrs. Schroeder gazed at him with worshipful eyes, and David knew she had missed the point. But he hoped that with her coming to his house they would become friends and that he would have an opportunity to explain further what he meant by that statement.

He returned to the clinic, walking via the canal and thinking about his morning. Accepting the position with Dr. Drake would probably mean there would be no more time for walks along the canal or down at the docks. He crossed over the canal and was surprised to see Otis Washburn was also strolling along Court Street. But what was really intriguing was that he had a woman on his arm. A very attractive one. The reporter did not see David. His attention was entirely engrossed by his lady friend. David felt a surge of relief, hoping that this meant that Washburn would not be pursuing Josephine. It wasn't as if he had any claims on her, and Josephine had even said that she was not interested in Washburn, but still, David hoped that this other woman would keep Mr. Washburn occupied.

Things hadn't been perfect the other night at the Clines', but at least Randolph had not kicked him out of the house or demanded that he leave his daughter alone. In fact, David enjoyed standing up to the man and relished the ensuing challenge. But if he accepted Drake's offer, no doubt the door would slam in his face. It was either the opportunity of a lifetime or the very thing that would ruin his life.

Josephine wrapped her muffler about her neck and stepped into the crisp air. She had just come from church services, and now she was on her way to the workhouse to visit with one of her wards. She had first met

Rosemary the day that David had held his clinic at the workhouse. She climbed the steps and entered the brick building, placed her cloak and muffler on a hook in the cloakroom, then proceeded down the long hall to the dorm where she was to meet Rosemary. She joined Rosemary on her meager cot to talk.

"How have you been feeling?"

"The baby moves a lot. But *gut* I am."

"I'm praying that your child will be strong like you."

The young German woman dipped her head and raised sad eyes. "Sometimes March seems far away. Other times I do not wish the day of birth to come. This child. How will I raise? I know not anything about being a mother."

"Neither do I. But if you love the child, that will be enough."

"True this is?"

"There is another person who can help you more than anyone. He can be a father to the baby."

Rosemary's eyes widened. She shook her head. "I need no man."

"You need this one. His name is Jesus."

"You speak of God." Rosemary smiled.

"Yes. Do you know Jesus?"

"No. But this I believe. You do. If you pray

for me. It helps."

Josie reached out and touched the younger woman. "I will pray. And I will pray that you will know Him as I do."

"Look!" Rosemary pointed out the bleak square window. "It snows!"

"Oh, my! Come!" Josie grabbed Rosemary's hand, and together they went to the window and watched the large flakes descend. As the snow blanketed Cincinnati, it seemed to cover its imperfections.

The large flakes piled up outside the clinic. Tom kept the fire going all afternoon, but once the snow started, the stream of patients lessened. At such a break, the clinic door blew open and David's new cook stepped inside.

"Whew. The snow's coming thick."

"I had hoped you would have headed home by now. I should have checked in on you," he returned in German.

"I'm on my way. I wanted to tell you that there's a stew on your stove."

"Did you make yourself a meal of it? That's part of the pay. You eat a portion of what you fix."

"But that's not right."

"It most certainly is. How are you going to find the time to cook for yourself? By the time you walk home, you'll be tired. It's the only way that this arrangement can work out for us. Now hurry over there and eat and be on your way."

Mrs. Schroeder glanced back outside. "If it wasn't coming down so hard, I'd stay and argue."

"Go."

She chuckled. "I'm going. I'm going."

Tom chuckled. "What was that all about?"

"Food."

"Ah!"

An hour later the snow was only lightly falling. It was so beautiful that it gave David a sudden inspiration.

"Can you close up here? I've an errand to run."

"Certainly."

David hurried out to make his arrangements. By the time he was finished, his mouth was watering for Mrs. Schroeder's stew. It was still warm and delicious. He set out a small bowl to cool for the cat who rubbed against his leg.

"It's as delicious as it smells. You're going to love this."

His clock struck seven. It was time. He put the bowl on the floor and dashed out the door, brimming with excitement. Within the hour he manned a horse-driven sleigh toward the Cline residence. He jumped down, secured the horse, and knocked. The servant invited him in to wait for Josephine.

"David." Josephine's laughter tinkled like the bells on the sleigh. "Look at you. You're all snowed on. Isn't it wonderful?"

"I thought it was cause for a celebration. Winter's first snow. Come look outside."

Josephine peered out and gasped with delight. "You brought a sleigh! What a thoughtful man you are. I'll just be a moment."

"Dress warm!" he called needlessly after her.

When she returned, David helped her into the sleigh and positioned a lap blanket across her legs. "Giddyap!"

The sleigh lurched. "Ooh! I haven't had this much fun since I was a child."

"Neither have I." David laughed. The snow felt cold and wet against his face. "I can't keep you out in this long, so let's enjoy it while we can."

The street was beautiful with its white carpet, gas lanterns, and other horses and sleighs. It was just the sort of thing that was wonderful enough to be impressed upon one's mind as a forever memory. "Oh, look! Everyone has the same idea."

Josephine studied him. "I wouldn't have

thought this snow would make you so happy. Didn't you say that it would halt progress on your project?"

"It does, but I was expecting it. Part of the reason that I am so happy is your father's wonderful suggestion and my full stomach."

"Mrs. Schroeder?"

"Yes. She cooked me up a hearty stew and seemed as pleased with our new arrangement as I am. It seems many things could be changing in my life."

"How is that?"

"Dr. Drake asked me if I wanted to become his personal assistant. Give up the clinic." As soon as the words were out, David wondered why he had divulged that bit of information. He had meant to keep it to himself while he considered it. It must have been the mood, the happiness bubbling over inside.

"But you love your work."

"I know. It's a difficult decision." He wished more than ever he hadn't brought it up. He didn't want to spoil things.

"I'll pray about it for you."

"Thank you."

"I had a good day also. Remember the pregnant girl from when you held the clinic at the workhouse?"

"Yes, I do."

"Rosemary is German, and she's teaching me some of the language. We had a nice meeting today. In fact, we were together when we saw the snow through her window." Josephine looked shy. "I was trying to tell her about Jesus."

"How did she respond?"

"She wants me to pray for her."

"That's a good start. I'm hoping to lead Mrs. Schroeder to God's throne. When I first met her and she almost died from that alleged curse, I begged God to save her, hoping that He would have a chance to win her soul. Then I forgot about her until I saw her son the other day dicing. I guess it was God's reminder. I know that when He's behind a thing, it will happen. It's not of my own doing. It's always God, pure and simple."

"But we still have to explain it to them."

"Yes. It all happens so naturally if it is of God."

"I'm happy to know about your faith in God. You mentioned that your parents were missionaries, but I did not know how it was with you and the Lord."

"It is well with me and the Lord. I am glad that we can talk of such things together."

By this time they had circled the city and returned outside the Clines' residence. Josephine's face and hair were wet, her cheeks rosy, and her eyes bright. She looked wonderful. "I wish our ride could go on, but I must get you inside to warm up. Doctor's orders."

Josephine clasped his arm with her mittens. "Thank you so much for this enchanting evening. I don't think I shall ever forget it. Please, do not get down. I'll be fine." She released him and jumped down before he could object. "Bye!" She waved.

A warmth churned inside David's chest. He waved back, then waited until she had disappeared inside the large, austere house. He could not remember when he had enjoyed himself so much. "Giddyap!"

CHAPTER 17

December days grew cold. Snow piled up. Mrs. Schroeder came whenever the weather permitted, and David made sure that she did not go hungry. Sometimes they dined together. He would read from his brown leather Bible and translate into German. Gradually the immigrant woman received a foundation of biblical truth. He anxiously watched for what the Lord would do with these seeds, confident God would work a miracle in her life.

His work brought satisfaction. His friendship with Josephine was burgeoning. Oftentimes they still disagreed in their discussions, and Randolph was still a touchy subject.

With an inward grin, he remembered how Randolph had reluctantly admitted that his relief from hemorrhoids had made him a new man, that he could even ride horseback again. He had offered to pay David for his medical services, but he had declined. Still, dinner at the Clines' oftentimes left David feeling that he had been weighed and found lacking.

Today David was eagerly anticipating a social engagement with Josephine. They were going Christmas shopping together. Mrs. Schroeder had even volunteered to spend her day making tea and chaperoning so Josephine could meet Gratuity. Women. They had such funny ideas. Being friends with Josephine was complicated. There were always the rules of propriety to keep in mind. Even though they were merely friends, her reputation needed guarding.

The idea of meeting Gratuity had stemmed from Josephine's remark that David was putting on weight since Mrs. Schroeder was cooking for him. When he replied that he was not fat compared to his cat, Josephine had become intrigued with the idea of his having a pet. This fascination increased until she had become adamant about meeting his cat. Jokingly he had told Mrs. Schroeder of his plans to bring Josephine to the clinic and introduce Gratuity. It was then the older woman had insisted that she prepare her apple strudel and tea for the special occasion and that he bring his young lady to his home where she would be their chaperone. Josephine had been delighted with the idea. And David was delighted over any event that would allow him to spend time with Josephine.

He knocked on the Clines' door. Mrs. Cline greeted him warmly and struck up a conversation until Josephine appeared. "Will you dine with us tonight, Doctor?" the older woman asked.

"Thank you for the invitation, but my cook is making me a strudel and insists that it must be eaten hot. In fact, she has offered to chaperone so that Josephine can sample it. Why don't you join us? We'd love to have you."

"Oh no. I wouldn't dream of intruding upon your afternoon."

"You're welcome to come, Mother."

"No. I've other things to attend to. But do come to dinner soon, Doctor."

"He will. I'll see to it."

David shrugged, and Mrs. Cline chuckled. "Have fun, dears."

As soon as they were outside, David joked, "If only Papa were so warmhearted."

Josephine bumped against him playfully. "Give him time. Minds, bodies, and hearts all take time to heal."

David swept off his hat and bowed deeply. "I salute you, Miss Poet Divine."

She smacked his arm. "Do stop and be serious. We need to think of a gift for —"

"Oh, no. I'm not choosing a gift for Papa."

"Rosemary at the workhouse. I thought maybe she'd like something for the baby."

"Ah. Little things, easy to carry. That is *gut.*"

"You are in fine fiddle today. But so am I. And I'm looking forward to seeing your home and meeting your fat cat."

"Mrs. Schroeder has promised to make it presentable and most importantly not to let the cat out."

Josephine said wistfully, "I wish I could speak German so I could relate to her. The language is hard to learn."

"Don't give up. Which reminds me. What should I give Mrs. Schroeder for Christmas? It's the perfect opportunity to give her something without her arguing about accepting charity."

"Oh, yes. I do remember how she refused my comforter."

"What comforter?"

Josie reddened. "Right after you told me that folks didn't like to take charity, Mother and I took her a comforter. Only, she refused it. That was the first time, I believe, that I thought maybe you weren't entirely wrong on every issue."

"And you never told me."

Josephine stopped abruptly. "I've got it! What we can get Mrs. Schroeder." David stumbled to a halt and tilted his head, waiting. "Charles told us his mother liked feather blankets. That's what they use in Germany."

"Perfect!" In his exuberance, David swept up Josephine and spun her around. When they stopped, her face shone and her gaze revealed an emotion that made David's heart squeeze. The discovery that Josephine was more than a friend overwhelmed him. He quickly withdrew. "I beg your pardon. I guess I got carried away." Her expression turned to one of confusion so he mumbled, "Come." Then snatching hold of her hand, he hurried them forward as if they were on their way to a fire.

Hours later the moment had been entirely forgotten. They trudged toward his living quarters, shopping weary. At the sight of home, his stomach growled. Josephine giggled.

David opened the door to the smell of apples, cinnamon, and the wood fire. Gratuity pranced around their feet.

"Oh, you adorable creature!" Josephine knelt.

"Careful, she's not used to strangers."

Scooping the cat up in her arms, Josephine only smiled at him then returned to scratching the cat's head. "What's your name, Beautiful?"

"Gratuity."

A slow look of recognition came over her features. "A patient?"

"Yes. And one of God's small blessings."

"God?" Mrs. Schroeder asked, repeating one of the few English words she recognized.

David spieled off a string of German, then turned back to Josie. "She welcomes us and wants us to sit and eat."

Josephine thanked Mrs. Schroeder and asked David to translate. They talked about how much Josephine's father liked Charles and how well he was doing. They chuckled over how fat David was getting, though he knew they were only kidding him.

When the conversation lagged, David wondered what Josephine was thinking about his meager apartment. His modest furnishings had never bothered him before. But now he wished to please her and regretted his negligence in making it homey or nice. The mixture of nearly broken-down furniture and odd assortments of masculine items had been haphazardly collected over the years. The only cheery things in the room were those with breath in them: Mrs. Schroeder, Josie, and Gratuity.

They invited Mrs. Schroeder to join them in their meal, but she insisted on serving. And then when it was time for Josie to leave, Mrs. Schroeder stayed to clean up.

On their way back to Josephine's house, she asked, "Do you think Mrs. Schroeder will accept a feather blanket?"

"I think she will. But how shall we accomplish it?"

"It can be a project for some of the women at the workhouse. I'll split the cost with you."

"I can pay for it. I know my place doesn't look like much. But I've got a bit of money stashed away. I've just never given any thought to houses or furniture or anything like that."

Josephine touched his sleeve. "Don't do this, David. I thought your little place was a perfect abode for such a person as yourself."

"Meaning?"

"Dedicated to your work, sacrificing your life for others."

"I suppose some people can have a piece of both worlds. You seem to. But I've never had a desire for things. I hope you realize that a man like me has nothing much to offer a woman except friendship."

"I could take offense at that remark, but knowing you as I do, I won't. I value our friendship above any other that I have. Will you just accept that? And will you accept me as I am? Father, mansion, and all?"

"How could I not?"

They had reached her home by this time. "Do come inside, and see Mother's reaction to these tiny baby things."

"I would love to, but I've committed myself to Dr. Drake this evening."

"Oh?"

David detected jealousy or hurt. "I'm sorry. I shouldn't have promised but —"

"No." She pushed his coat front, and her voice softened. "It's fine. You go ahead. There will be other times. I'll let you know about the feather blanket."

He clasped her hand and squeezed. "Thanks, Josie." Her face reddened at the endearing form that he had used of her name. And David's heart warmed another notch toward her.

David slipped into the room filled with his medical colleagues. Dr. Drake had already started to explain the reason for calling them all together.

"As the eye infirmary remains a success, aside from much-needed funds, I'm looking for volunteers to learn the art of this particular surgery. It's taking up so much of my time that I need other physicians to fill in."

David squirmed in his chair, grateful at least that this meeting had nothing to do with the doctor's previous offer to him. Putting that issue aside, he considered Drake's appeal. David didn't wish to spend his valuable time at the hospital. He enjoyed the practice that he had at the clinic. Of course it would be helpful to learn a new technique or two, but not at the expense of turning the clinic over to his assistant.

After the general plea and following lecture, Drake served hot apple cider and mixed with his guests to round up recruits.

"So, David, are you ready to learn eye surgery?"

"I'm ready to *learn,* Sir. But the way things are at the clinic right now, I cannot afford to spend the time at the hospital. Perhaps someone else is more inclined —"

"Nonsense. You should always be willing to learn new things, David. You must not grow stale."

"But I have my mornings doing field work already, and Tom Langdon and I have our hands full at the clinic."

"Think about it. I know I can count on you. Come to the hospital in a day or two, and let me know. And we need to talk about the other. Soon." He walked away toward another young physician.

David sighed, said his farewells, and headed home. It had been a day of revelation, and he had much to think about, pray about. First, there came the realization that Josie was more than a friend. And now this.

CHAPTER 18

Josie watched David balance the awkward package. His face was flushed from the cold and exertion. His blue eyes shone. They crossed the canal and headed down Thirteenth Street to Mrs. Schroeder's apartment.

"I hope she accepts it," Josie worried out loud.

"Don't worry. I know how to handle her."

"I suppose you do. You can be very charming when you set your mind to it."

"Ah, yes. That's what everyone calls me, the charming doctor."

"Are you sure you don't mean 'the eccentric doctor'?"

"Exactly," he said with a wry smile.

Josie chuckled. She wished Father had agreed to invite David to Christmas dinner and feared he would be offended when he learned he wasn't invited. She knew David had family and wondered if he would be traveling north to visit them. She was thankful they had planned this outing to present Mrs. Schroeder with the feather blanket. The crisp air stung her lungs. She buried her face in her fur muff.

"Cold?"

"Walking keeps me warm, but don't you think the weather's turning colder?"

"And darker. Could snow again."

Josie fondly remembered their sleigh ride. "Have you visited Mrs. Schroeder since you hired her? Do you think she's staying warm enough?"

"I haven't called on her. But she claims she is. Dropping in today unannounced was a good idea."

"As long as she's at home."

David peered over the package at her. "You're kind of cute when your forehead wrinkles like that."

She wrinkled her nose at him, too.

"Here we are. Ready?"

Josie nodded. If not for David, she would have been afraid to approach Mrs. Schroeder with another gift offering even though the woman had acted warmly toward her that day at David's home. When one couldn't communicate in the same language, it was hard.

"Don't forget to translate everything to me."

"Nudge me if I don't."

"Maybe I'll pinch you."

"You do, and you had better run fast."

She giggled. Together they climbed the steps. David knocked on the door, and it slowly cracked open.

"Doctor. Come in," Mrs. Schroeder said in German.

Josephine followed David into the warm apartment. "Merry Christmas." David grinned, placing the wrapped package on the table, and then translating for Josephine.

"What is this?"

"Open it."

Mrs. Schroeder unwrapped the paper. She placed her palms against her pink cheeks in astonishment. "I am so ashamed." Tears pooled in her eyes.

Josephine and David looked at each other in dismay. Mrs. Schroeder spoke again. "What? What is she saying?" Josie asked with concern.

"She says it was cruel and prideful of her to say that she preferred feather quilts. But so thoughtful of you to make this."

"Tell her that the women at the workhouse helped. And be sure she knows that it is from you, too."

David and Mrs. Schroeder exchanged sentences. Finally, the woman approached Josephine. "Thank you, Miss Cline," she said in broken English. "Very lovely you are."

Josephine looked at her in amazement. "You are learning English?"

"My gift to you."

Through the blur of stinging tears Josephine saw David cross his arms and gaze proudly at Mrs. Schroeder. "What does she mean, David?"

"She wanted me to teach her some English. It was her gift to you."

Swiping back her pooling tears, Josie stepped forward and gave the older woman a warm hug. After they separated, both dabbed at their cheeks.

"Tell her that I am also learning some German words."

David did. Mrs. Schroeder replied, and he chuckled. "I believe she is matchmaking. She suggested that I should be your instructor."

Josie squeaked, "Matchmaking?"

"I'll explain to her about our friendship later. I'm sure she'll question me all about you again."

Swiping at some fresh tears over the way he had scoffed at the idea, Josie nodded.

Mrs. Schroeder motioned for them to sit and began hustling to prepare them something warm to drink. When the older woman's back was turned, Josie whispered to David. "The place seems snug and warm. I believe she's doing all right."

Later when they left Mrs. Schroeder's building, the snow was falling. "This makes it seem like Christmas," Josephine said, remembering their November sleigh ride.

"I believe after this I won't be able to watch it snow without thinking of you."

Josie smiled. He could always read her mind. Sometimes he was so sweet. "Are you going home for Christmas?" she asked.

"You mean to visit family?"

Josie nodded.

"No. I cannot get away right now. Dr. Drake's got some newfangled ideas, and I'm so busy I can hardly find the time for anything." He sounded resentful.

"What sort of newfangled ideas?"

"He wants me to learn to do eye surgery."

"That sounds like a good idea."

"He needs surgeons who will give him a break at the hospital. But I'm busy enough with my own work at the clinic. Still, how can I refuse him? It's an opportunity of a lifetime, and I owe him so much already." He shrugged. "All of Drake's ideas are good. It's just that he has his hands in so many different things, and he seems to accomplish everything so well. I feel like I'm letting him down, lazy or something."

"Nonsense!" Josie frowned. "How can you say that? You do not have to be like him to be special. Can't you see how unique your ministry is?"

"Sometimes I wonder. My parents accomplished so much, dedicating their lives to missionary work. Dr. Drake's achievements in medicine and science are astonishing. The whole world benefits, while I accomplish so little. If I did do the eye surgery and work at the hospital, it would fit in better with his plans for me and his other offer."

"Being his personal assistant?"

"Yes. But it also eases me out of my clinic work. It's a tough decision. And I know being Drake's personal assistant would not endear me to your father."

Josie grew angry over David's belittling of himself. He really believed that he was not meeting others' expectations. He was an excellent physician and had made a difference in many lives. "You've been teaching me to think for myself. Now I want you to do the same. You are a special person, talented in the ways that God created you.

Your ambitions may be different from any other man's, but they are the ones you were designed for. You must use your talents accordingly and only be concerned that you do your best and not how you measure up with any other person's expectations of you."

David looked down at her with surprise. "Not even your expectations?"

"Be serious."

"I am."

"Then you are overly concerned with pleasing others."

"I will think about that, Josephine. In the meantime, tell me what you are doing for Christmas."

"Nothing special. We will go to church. Mother will cook. Father will read the Christmas story."

"I have an idea, but I'm not sure if it will fit in with your plans." Josephine listened. "If the weather stays this cold and the canal freezes solid, maybe we could find some time on Christmas Day after your family festivities to go ice skating."

"If the weather holds, I will make the time. It sounds delightful."

"Good." They looked up at the Clines' residence. Fresh snow covered the walk and windowsills. "Thank you for everything you did for Mrs. Schroeder."

"I enjoyed it so much. I'll see you on Christmas afternoon then, if the weather holds."

David squeezed her mitten-clad hand and smiled warmly. "Bye, Josie."

She paused outside her door and turned back to watch him walk away. The back of his coat was white from snow. She looked down at their footsteps in the snow. This man was special. She hoped he would come to appreciate that.

Christmas Eve afternoon, Mrs. Schroeder cooked David a turkey dinner.

"You are still here. I am glad. I wanted to wish you a Happy Christmas."

"That is why I waited. I have a gift for you."

David took the rectangular package and examined it. Carefully he unwrapped the paper. It was a small wooden box, intricately carved.

"It is from the homeland. I thought it was something you could use."

"I will cherish it. Before you go, may I read the Christmas story to you?"

"Yes. I was wondering if you would. Some of the things you have told me have my curiosity."

With Gratuity curled up at his feet, David read the story and translated from Luke 2:10–11. "And the angel said unto them, Fear not: for, behold, I bring you good tidings of great joy, which shall be to all people. For unto you is born this day in the city of David a Saviour, which is Christ the Lord."

"You are my savior," Mrs. Schroeder said. "You are an angel."

"No. Just a human. There is only one Savior."

"His power is strong? You used His power to break the neighbor's curse?"

David hardly knew how to form his reply. He did not want to lie. But he knew she was not ready to hear about the frog's help quite yet, even though he realized someday he would need to disclose his secret.

"His power is stronger than any evil. It is enough that the crucified Jesus was brought back to life again. Just as you can be if you only have faith."

"Tell me about faith," she said.

David explained how faith in Christ saves mankind from sin. And when Mrs. Schroeder asked if this Jesus would take her side or her neighbor's, he had to explain that God is not prejudiced.

"That was a good story. Now I must go

and prepare Christmas for Charles."

"Thank you for taking the time to listen. And for this gift. Tell Charles Merry Christmas for me." He wished that she had better understood the true meaning of Christmas.

"I will. Now you must eat your meal before it gets cold."

He nodded and breathed a prayer, releasing this special woman over to the Lord's care.

CHAPTER 19

Dr. Drake's Christmas party caused David to feel lonely. Though it was good to spend time with his colleagues and friends, Dr. Drake's usual inspirational speech only left David feeling frustrated. Until he met Josephine, he had lingered on every word from Drake — every idea inspired him. David wondered if this let-down feeling came because he had been depending upon Drake more than God. Something Josephine had said that day they visited Mrs. Schroeder had been nibbling at his mind. Something about he and God choosing his course and being content with it.

At one point in his life, David had thought he had done that. It was when he made the choice to remain in the States and go into medicine rather than return to the missionary field with his parents. Of course, for a time they had expected him to return to them with his medical experience and join their work. But he hadn't felt led to do that. That was when he had felt confident he was on the right track with his life and following God's leading, even though it had been a sacrifice to be without family. When had he turned the reins over to Dr. Drake?

It was complicated. Drake was his teacher, his mentor — an intelligent, inspiring leader. Was this urge for independence the result of his association with Josephine or was it God's leading? The last time he had experienced such desperation, he had chosen a Bible study in Ecclesiastes. Seeking that special closeness with God, he got out his Bible and turned to the same passage.

He read about the beauty and burden of man's labor and listened carefully for God's Spirit to gently whisper direction. When he came to the middle of chapter four, the words gripped him. "Two are better than one; because they have a good reward for their labour. For if they fall, the one will lift up his fellow: but woe to him that is alone when he falleth; for he hath not another to help him up. Again, if two lie together, then they have heat: but how can one be warm alone?"

Josephine's concerned voice came to him. *Do you think Mrs. Schroeder is staying warm enough?* Other thoughts tumbled through his mind. *Friends help each other. Mates keep each other warm. Two are better than one.* Now he really felt lonely.

"Lord, I feel like I am floundering. What am I missing? Do I need to make a change in my career? Am I not spending enough time with You? Is Josephine confusing my life? Why am I so drawn to her? What are You trying to tell me? I do not want to go down the wrong road. I want to stay in Your will."

Gratuity's mewing interrupted his thoughts. "What is it, Girl?" He opened his eyes. The cat had a Christmas gift for him. It lay at his feet. "Gratuity! You take that mouse outside." But the cat snapped up its unappreciated offering and ran under the bed.

Josephine watched through the frosty pane for David. She hadn't long to wait until she saw his straight, fit form bounding up the road. She quickly plunged into her cloak, grabbed her skates, and headed outside. "Merry Christmas!"

He smiled broadly. "I could not come empty-handed on Christmas Day. Will you accept this small token of our friendship?"

"Of course. But I have something for you, too. Shall we open them upon our return?"

David nodded, and she hurried back into the house to leave the package. When she returned, he was whistling.

"Let me carry those." He took her skates. "How was your day so far?"

"Lovely. And neither Mother nor Father could fault my eagerness to go skating, though both were concerned about my safety."

"Don't worry. I won't let anything happen to you."

"That's what I assured them. How was your day?"

David shrugged. "Festive enough. Only I could see how lonely Dr. Drake is. He still misses his wife. Somehow the loneliness seeped over onto me."

"Well, I shan't give you time to think about that any more today. Oh, look!"

There were several couples on the ice. The women's long, full skirts made a pretty picture, like winter flowers. Everyone was bundled. Many glided gracefully while some children were learning the art. Josephine clapped. "I'm so excited."

When they reached the ice, David offered, "If you let me help you with those skates, you won't have to sit on the cold ground."

"All right." She slipped her skirt just high enough for David to assist her. Still kneeling in front of her, he suggested, "Take hold of my shoulder so you don't lose your balance."

She used his shoulder to steady herself. The moment she touched him, it felt as if the day had warmed at least fifteen degrees. His touch was gentle, capable, that of a doctor tending a patient. Yet it also seemed personal the way he helped her slip into the skates.

He made the final adjustments and helped her to a nearby tree. "Hang on here while I put mine on."

She giggled as he sank to the ground and his manner changed from gentle to awkward motions, much tugging and grunting. "You must not have much confidence in my abilities by the way you've attached me to this tree."

"Just remembering your promise to your father. Until I'm rigged up, I don't want you skating off by yourself. All done." He stood up and offered his hand. "Ready to give it a try?"

"Let's go."

They clomped through the frozen grass, which was easy to walk in, but the drop-off to the ice was a bit trickier. David jumped down first. His legs went out from him, and he landed on his rump. She giggled, and he quickly jumped up and steadied himself. "Your turn." He positioned his heels together so he wouldn't slide away and grabbed her by the waist to ease her down onto the ice. They teetered a bit then found their balance. Taking her hand again, he led her toward the center of the ice. "You are very good."

"Thank you. So are you, Doctor."

Josephine loved the opportunity to hold David's hand — to bump up against his strong, solid body. It made her feel feminine and protected. And the way he kept smiling at her made her feel cherished. She only hoped he cared about her in a special way and that it was not all her imagination.

The afternoon was even more wonderful than she had imagined it might be. She wished it could go on forever. But eventually the crowd thinned and the wind picked up. It would be futile to pretend that she wasn't cold and her legs and feet weren't tired and wobbly.

Maneuvering off the ice was a little easier than getting on. David climbed up the embankment and reached back to easily pull her up onto the snowy grass. They returned to the tree, and this time Josephine backed up against it while David removed her skates. "Are your feet frozen?"

"Yes," she admitted.

"We'll take a hackney. I fear I kept you out too long."

She watched him remove his own skates. "It was so fun. I don't regret it."

"You are a good sport." He held her hand again. "Come. Let's catch that one."

Inside the hackney, Josephine shivered.

"You poor thing. Here, come close." David placed his arm around her shoulders and drew her into his warmth. He whispered into her ear, "Two are better than one. Ecclesiastes."

His breath was warm and sweet against her cheek. She turned toward him. He was gazing intently at her, and she could not look away. Slowly he lowered his face. He was going to kiss her. Her heart raced. There was no time to consider what it all might mean. She felt drawn to him. The kiss was like his touch had been. Gentle. He pulled away and smiled. She blushed. He touched her cheek. "Merry Christmas, Josie. I shall always remember the fun we had together today."

She took a deep breath. "David, I . . . me, too."

"Warm enough?"

"What? Oh." She smiled, embarrassed. "Yes."

He leaned back in the carriage, his arm still around her possessively, and neither of them spoke again until they had reached her house. She wasn't sure what to make of it. And she was afraid to stir, lest he remove his arm and the dream would disappear like vapor. But when the carriage lurched to a stop, he moved away from her and descended, then helped her down. His hands against her waist did not linger, and she wondered if he was regretting their kiss. His gaze did not meet hers.

"You must come in. We need to exchange our gifts."

"Are you sure?"

She looked up at him. "Yes. And you will join me for some warm cider."

"Sounds heavenly." He was looking at her with that strange look again, like he had just before he kissed her. She swallowed and nodded, and they went into the house.

Soon they were seated in a small sitting area with a gigantic fire and two steaming cups of cider. After several warming swallows, they set them aside and turned their attention to opening their gifts.

Josephine caressed the cover of *The Adventures of Captain Bonneville.* "I'm so excited. I shall start to read this tonight."

"I wasn't sure, but I thought you would

enjoy something adventuresome since you attended the lecture on Indian treaties. There's an inscription."

She turned the beginning pages until she found it. *I look forward to a discussion when you have finished.*

David fumbled with his gift. It was so fragile and tiny. Finally, the paper fell away. His eyes lit, and he smiled as he held the delicate glass snowflake by its gold thread. "It's perfect."

She was touched by his tone. "When I saw it, it reminded me of you."

"It's a perfect symbol of our . . ." It sounded like he had a lump in his throat. ". . . of our friendship."

She ventured, "Many faceted. It's very special. Like you, David."

"Thank you." He gazed at it in his palm, caressing it with his finger.

Long after he was gone, and she was alone in her room with the book he had given her, the memory of it lingered in her mind.

CHAPTER 20

After Christmas David decided to receive eye surgery instruction from Dr. Drake. Aside from a flood of patients at the clinic, there were now sketches and notes to pour over. Josephine was pushed to the back of his life for several reasons. First, he knew he had advanced their relationship to another level when he had kissed her, and it frightened him. So he put off seeing her, feeling unfamiliar with this new stage of their relationship.

The matter was so uncomfortable to consider that when Dr. Drake had once again confronted him about learning eye surgery, this time he had jumped at the chance to bury himself in his work.

As the days turned into weeks, he was surprised that Josephine had not taken the initiative to call on him at the clinic. During those times that he thought about her, he hoped that she was well and wondered if she was avoiding him. Maybe she also regretted the kiss and did not feel attracted to him the way he felt attracted to her. If so, this time apart would do them both good.

And so it had gone until one day in mid-January when Mrs. Cline stopped in at his clinic and scolded him soundly. "I would think when one's friend has pneumonia one would visit her. Especially when one is a doctor."

"Josie?"

"She's been very ill. But worst of all, she thinks you've abandoned her."

David grabbed his coat and yelled over his shoulder, "Tom, take over here." Nearly pushing Mrs. Cline out the clinic's front door, he asked, "Has she seen a doctor?"

"Of course. How else would I know that she has pneumonia?"

"But this is a very serious thing." He of all people knew how pneumonia could snuff out a person's life. He panicked at the thought of his Josephine being in the clutches of death. "Why didn't you contact me sooner?" They climbed into Mrs. Cline's carriage.

"Josie wouldn't let me."

He dipped his head in his hands and mumbled, "I've been so busy, too busy."

"She's over the worst of it. Don't fret so."

He relaxed a bit. "Thank you for coming for me."

"She doesn't know I've gone for you," Mrs. Cline said curtly.

When they arrived, she led the way to the sitting room where Josephine reclined on a couch ensconced in blankets. Her head was propped up on a pillow, her hair spilling around her face and shoulders. She looked angelic. He drew in a breath and held it. Mrs. Cline left them, and he rushed forward.

"Josie, I'm so sorry."

"David? You finally came."

"You have every reason to be miffed. I didn't know you were ill. I was just so busy learning eye surgery, and the clinic's been busy."

She waved. "Don't do this." But she did not say anything else. She just gazed at him with a betrayed expression. "I missed you."

So many emotions flooded over David. He was angry with himself for abandoning her. He felt protective and wanted to scoop her up and hold her to his chest. He wanted to examine her and make sure that she was improving. "Why didn't you send for me?"

"I thought you would come. Every day I thought you would come. I thought . . . we were friends."

He clasped her hand. A tear slid down his cheek. "I'm a fool." The clock chimed. "And I'm late." He jumped to his feet. "Surgery. I'm supposed to be at the hospital. When I heard about you, I forgot all about it. It can't be helped. I have to go. But I'll be back."

Her voice saddened. "Go then."

"I'm sorry."

Josephine watched him leave. Then she pulled the blanket over her head and wept. The day they had gone skating, she thought he had shown signs of devotion. But he hadn't called, and then she had gotten so sick. She'd kept waiting for him to come. He didn't. Then she had remembered how he had told her that he was lonely, missing his family. And she wondered if he had only shown such affection that Christmas Day because he had been feeling weak and lonely.

At first she had resolved not to let it bother her, but it did. At times she thought she could wait for him to realize how much he needed her. There was no doubt anymore in her own mind that she needed him. But at other times she grew weary of waiting and sometimes even angry enough that she wished he would stay away. But then he came to call upon her. And now she was even more confused.

Once she'd recuperated, she was going to have to help the doctor discover his feelings for her. She was sure she had seen evidence of the beginning of love in his eyes. Yes, she would think about that.

The rest of January taxed David's patience. First of all, he was still busy at the hospital. Secondly, Tom Langdon had gotten the idea that as soon as he finished his internship, he was going to go to the backwoods to practice medicine. Then David would be left alone again. Thirdly, the only times he could see Josephine was when he called on her at her home, where Randolph Cline always made him feel unwelcome. It was as if he blamed her illness on him.

One particular visit remained vivid in David's memory. Josie had expressed regret over falling behind on her German lessons, and he had offered his services.

"I can give you a lesson or two."

"But what would you teach me?" Her expression had teased.

"How about the word for good health? *Gut Gesundheit.*" She repeated it several times. "Special lady — *speziell Dame.*"

Josie practiced, then surprised him by asking, "How do you say 'handsome doctor'?"

"*Stattlich Doktor.* You may say that as often as you like." It had been the perfect opportunity to lead into the word for love, but he had lost his nerve. Instead he remembered the sadness that had filled her brown eyes when his next word was *friends.*

After that and with the general course of events, he and Josie had regressed in their relationship, back to the more comfortable stages of friendship they had earlier experienced. The door to a deeper relationship had closed. With time, calling on her had become perfunctory. It suited him most days. Though, sometimes, he had to admit there was a longing that he had to stifle. He had become expert at doing that and at covering up his emotions.

With February came sadness. One morning David went to the docks to check on the homeless. He discovered the dead body of the black man who had been found ill during one of their workdays. It deeply moved him, for the man had always been so sweet and thankful each time David called upon him. He trudged through his morning heavy of heart, finally finding himself at Josephine's door.

"David. What's wrong? You look awful." Josephine drew him inside.

"I found a friend at the docks this morning, frozen. My house is nice and warm and cozy, and my friend was frozen."

Tears welled up in Josie's eyes. "Oh, David, I'm so sorry."

"Sometimes the weight of death is heavy."

She nodded, her eyes moist. "I cannot even imagine how you must feel."

They sat in silence for a long while. Eventually, he said, "I must go. I just needed someone."

"Two are better than one," she said, repeating what he had once told her.

"Especially when the other one is you," he replied.

Josephine finally convinced her mother she was well enough to resume her visits to the workhouse.

"I almost didn't recognize you," Josie told Rosemary. "You've gotten so —"

"Fat. The word is fat."

Josie giggled at the young woman's expression. "All pregnant women look roundly beautiful. Is there anything I can pray about for you?"

"I worry for the baby's birth. A proper home I need to find."

"I'm sure God has a plan for you." Josie squeezed the woman's hand. "We just need

216

to seek it."

As Josie worked, she was reminded that physically she was weaker, thinner. But she was confident that her strength would return. Many people didn't survive pneumonia. She was fortunate. If she weren't so tired, she would stop by the clinic. Wouldn't David be surprised to see her out and about?

Their time together had become rather dull and routine. Before her illness, they had done many exciting things together. She wondered now what she could do to spice things up, to jolt him out of his complacency, to move their relationship forward again. She intended to look over her list when she got home. She needed a plan that would grab David's attention.

CHAPTER 21

Josephine reclined and read the perfectly penned list of things her friendship with David could offer him:

We both share the desire to help others
Cooking and domestic abilities
Encourage him in Christian faith
Feminine appeal — attraction toward each other

Then she read the note added at the bottom, her mother's words: Demonstrate in ways that he can understand.

She thought she had worked at each of these points. Was she missing a point, or should she expand one of the points she had already listed? She brewed over it for at least an hour, trying this or that in her mind and considering the consequences.

The point about cooking abilities didn't even apply anymore. By persuading him to hire Mrs. Schroeder, her father had cunningly undermined one of her drawing points. How about intellectual stimulation? She grinned. It was something that any man in her life would need to appreciate. There was *The Adventures of Captain Bonneville* he had gotten her for Christmas. She had finished reading it. She could invite him over to discuss the book.

She glanced over the list again. *Attraction toward each other.* David didn't seem to really notice her anymore. She would change her appearance. With her illness, her skin had paled causing her freckles to stand out on her face. Perhaps she would try egg whites and go for that glazed effect that was so popular. A new hat wouldn't do for an indoor book discussion, but she could get one for another time. She had always been rather plain and conservative. Maybe she needed to try something more frilly, something to shock his sensibilities, make him see her as a woman. A new scent! The one she had always used, lavender, why she couldn't even smell it on herself any longer. She had heard that spiced rose water was all the rage.

With anticipation she put her plan into action, and finally the night of the anticipated book discussion arrived. Judging from the range of emotions displayed on David's face after he had entered the room, Josephine thought her plan might be working. He certainly appeared to be noticing her as a woman. First there had been surprise, then puzzlement, and now his face seemed to glow of pleasure or something likewise agreeable.

"My, you are dressed festively tonight," he said.

"When one's father is in textiles, it doesn't look good to dress shabbily."

"On the contrary, you look up to the occasion." He leaned closer, then frowned.

"What is wrong?"

"Have you changed your fragrance?"

Josephine felt her face heat. "Spiced rose water. It's all the rage."

"It's nice. But I really loved the lavender. I associated it with you. I'm relieved to see you have some color. When I first entered the room, I was concerned for your health. You looked so pale."

"You don't say."

"Now I've offended you. I didn't mean to. It's just that I've grown accustomed to you, or thought I knew you, and tonight I feel as if I'm sitting with a stranger."

"Do you find this new person interesting?"

"Absolutely charming."

She leaned close. *"Danke."*

Shock covered his face again. "What else have you done?" His voice was fatherly, chastising.

She jerked away and straightened her back. "You find something else to criticize?"

"Never. Only I loved your freckles, Josie. And well, your face looks glossy."

"Egg whites. Plautus says a woman without paint is like food without salt." She gave an exasperated look. "You certainly are stuffy."

"I am not. Why do you think you have to change your looks? You were plenty salty before."

"I was dull."

"Hah!" He threw his head back for a good laugh. "You have never been dull, Josie. Goodness, I'd only begun to feel comfortable and safe around you."

"Maybe I don't want you to feel comfortable and safe. Anyway, I invited you over to discuss literature not to discuss my personal appearance."

"Very well, forgive me. Let's see, we've already discussed Plautus. Washington Irving was in store for tonight, was he not?"

"He was."

"I shall let you begin our discussion." He

leaned back and continued to watch her with disconcerting awareness, and a tinge of shock and amusement.

She squirmed. "I find his descriptions of the Indians fascinating."

"This does not surprise me. I do, too. He does help us to see their personalities; each tribe was very different."

"I liked the Flatheads because it sounded like they were polite, peaceable, and treated everyone with respect," she said.

"Aren't they the ones who loved to race horses and gamble? As I recall, your folks didn't find it amusing when those dice rolled out of my pocket onto the dining room table."

She smiled. "And you knocked over your drink and stained Mother's cloth."

"She forgave me."

Josie reasoned. "To the Flatheads it was merely recreation. Everyone has to have recreation."

"True. What you said about showing respect, I like that. Everyone deserves that kind of treatment."

"I imagine you learned that from your parents."

"Yes. Did I ever tell you that Claire's parents were killed by the Indians?"

"No. What happened?"

"The Wyandots. It was when they were being pushed off their land. Mother says she forgave them. It was all very tragic. Just like any war."

"I felt sorry about the way things turned out for the Wyandots."

"My aunt's friend knew Tecumseh."

"Really?"

"It's a long story."

"Please, I would love to hear it."

When he had finished, she said, "It's a sad story. I didn't want this to be a sad evening."

"What did you want it to be, Josie? Seems like you went to a great deal of trouble to get my attention. What are you trying to tell me?"

She shrugged. "Only that I'd like to get more reaction out of you."

"I have been predictable, haven't I?"

"The *stattlicher Doktor* has been very predictable lately. He does not seem to be the same man who showed up at my doorstep with a sleigh. I thought perhaps I was at fault, that I was boring you."

"Oh, Josie. Never. It is all my fault. I've intentionally pushed my feelings for you away."

"What feelings, David?"

"Fond ones."

She waited, but he did not expound. She

had given him every opportunity to express his affection for her. But if there was to be any kind of romantic relationship between them, he would have to be able to express his heart and be willing to open up to her. It seemed like she had done all the chasing in this relationship. Well, she would not propose to him! His reluctance suddenly made her angry, weary. "Perhaps you can tell me about them another time, *stattlicher Doktor.* Suddenly I'm feeling tired."

David stood. "I understand. I've had an enjoyable evening. Thank you for making it special. I really will try harder to be a better . . ."

It was as if he knew it would anger her to say the *friend* word tonight so he did not finish his sentence. It hung there between them, unfinished. She took pity on him. "I know, David. Another time then."

David did not hail a hackney. He needed to walk and think about Josie's strange behavior. He still couldn't believe how she had arrayed herself in such an extreme manner with the glossy face and the rose water. Didn't she know that he loved her just the way she was?

Loved her? She had nearly caused him to admit his love for her. Why hadn't he? She had transformed from alluring to angry, practically tossing him out the door. He felt like she had not only dismissed him, but dismissed them. What if this time, she let him go for good?

It was what he deserved. He was predictable, boring, standoffish, and a whole lot of other words that she might have flung at him if he had stayed around much longer.

Stattlicher Doktor. She'd called him that twice. But the second time he had felt like the hatchet was going to fall on his neck any moment. She had mocked him, her mouth twisted as if she had a bad taste in it. Was that what he was becoming to her? A bad taste? A disappointment? Heaven forbid. As soon as he got home, he was going to fall on his knees and pray this through. He did not want to lose Josie. He could not bear it. Whatever it took, he would make things right between them again.

CHAPTER 22

Josie held Rosemary's clammy hand and stroked her forehead. "Everything is going to be fine. Be strong, Dear. The doctor is on his way."

"Pray." Rosemary groaned. "Please."

Josephine gladly slid to her knees beside the woman's bed. This was the first time she had been with a woman who was delivering a baby. Although a midwife was preparing to deliver the baby in case David didn't arrive in time, Josephine had also been called at Rosemary's request. Now Josephine trembled inside at the woman's pain and panicky eyes. Yet she tried to remain calm and reassuring. To do this she focused on her faith.

"Dear Lord. We have come to You before regarding this little one who will soon be born into this world. We pray that You will bring the baby safe and whole and protect this mother and ease her pain."

"Hello, ladies."

"Doctor."

"David." Relief filled Josie's voice. Although she had not seen David for a week, since the night she had made a fool of herself, she welcomed the sight of him now. Fear for Rosemary clutched her heart, making the mixed emotions she had been feeling over David seem trivial in comparison.

"Help me, Doctor. Please."

"Of course. Try not to worry, Rosemary. Who is going to give me a hand here?" He looked at Josephine.

She jerked away her gaze and pointed at the woman who would serve as his assistant. "She is." Then Josephine turned back to Rosemary. "I'll be just beyond the door, praying. The doctor is very capable."

A quick glance up at David revealed his warm expression. She gave a nod and left the room. Outside the closed door, Josie paced for what seemed like hours. Her thoughts ranged from worries over Rosemary's welfare to the state of her relationship with David.

It actually hurt to be in his presence and not be able to express the love she felt for him.

"Josie? Has the baby arrived?"

"Oh, Mother. I'm glad you're here. I don't

know. It's been so long."

"Sometimes it takes awhile for babies to find their way into the world."

A tear slid down Josie's cheek.

"Don't be troubled. Rosemary is in God's hands."

"No, it's not that. It's just David." She bit her lip to keep it from trembling.

"What has he done?"

"It's what he hasn't done."

"Oh." Mrs. Cline drew her daughter into an embrace. "All I can say is he doesn't know the joy he's missing not making you his own."

Josie hiccuped. A baby's cry filled the air. She covered her mouth and giggled through her tears. Her mother hugged her again, and Josie found herself crying and laughing at the same time. "I hope Rosemary is all right."

David's female assistant stuck her head out of the room, face all smiles. "We have us a little boy. The doctor's finishing up."

"How is Rosemary?"

"Fine."

Josie blotted her tears away and waited for the door to reopen. Finally she and her mother were invited into the room.

Slowly they approached the bed. Cradled in Rosemary's arms lay a red wrinkled infant with fuzzy blond hair. The baby's eyes were closed.

"Oh," Josie whispered. "How tiny and perfect." She lifted moist eyes to Rosemary. "I can see already that you are going to make a good mother."

"If only a decent home I had for him." As if she knew what Josie would say, the new mother added, "I remember. Just do my best."

"Trusting God helps," David added. "You have a fine boy."

Josie jerked at the sound of David's voice so near her ear.

"Doctor is right. Miss Josephine trusts God for me. It helps."

David gave instructions to the woman who had assisted him, then said, "Looks like I'm done here." He whispered to Josie, "May I speak with you in private?"

Josie glanced at him hesitantly. "I'll be right back, Rosemary."

"Sleepy, I am."

Outside the room, David asked, "How are you doing?"

"Exhausted. My first baby."

"Really? From what I could see, you were just what Rosemary needed."

"God is Who she really needs. But I won't give up on her."

He squeezed her hand. "I've got to get to the hospital. But I'd like to see you soon. Tonight? We need to talk."

"Yes."

"Get some rest."

David was relieved that the delivery had gone well. As he walked back to the clinic, Josephine's remark about Rosemary needing God kept playing in his mind, strengthening his resolve to have another talk with Mrs. Schroeder. In fact, he would pop his head inside his apartment now in hopes of catching her. He hadn't spoken with her in days. Then he would check in at the clinic. His thoughts briefly turned to his assistant. He wanted to tell Tom how much he needed him and try to encourage him to stay at the clinic.

"Doctor. See I've cooked you a hot stew for such a cold, windy day."

"Smells delicious! And I'm ravenous. Just delivered a baby."

"How wonderful." Her expression full of awe for several long moments slowly changed to teasing. "Shouldn't you be having your own babies soon? Miss Cline is a good candidate for you."

"If I go and marry, you might have to find another job. And I would miss you."

"Perhaps. But God provides."

"What?" David's head jerked around. He was surprised at the woman's confession.

"Your God provides. You always say this."

"Do you believe it?"

"All these days I watch you. Now I know what you say is true."

"The woman who had the baby, she needs a miracle. She needs a home and a job so that she can bring the child up properly."

"Does she not think that God will provide?"

"She trusts in Josephine's prayers but doesn't pray herself. She doesn't know Jesus. Let's put it this way: It's the difference between being a friend of a friend of the king or being a friend of the king himself."

"Oh." She sounded as if she was understanding for the first time.

"Would you like for this Jesus to be your friend and companion, to save you?"

Mrs. Schroeder nodded. "I know I sin. I hate my neighbor. But if what you say is all true, then I must not hate her. I cannot change. I hate her."

"This is true, but you do not need to worry about it. Jesus will help you to forgive her."

"There is much to forgive. Especially her

cursing me with the frog. I could have died."

"I have a confession. I should have told you long ago. The curse was not real."

"How can you say that? You saw the frog yourself."

"Yes, I did. We became friends that morning during my walk to your home. He was in my pocket. He helped me trick you so that you would get better."

Her eyes narrowed, and she shook her head. "*Nein*. It was the potion."

"The medicine made you heave. I tricked you. But only because I cared and didn't want you to be sick." David watched a myriad of emotions flicker across the German woman's face, including anger and doubt. He quickly added, "You didn't know about Jesus. I know it was wrong to pretend, but I thought that if I could save your body, God might be able to save your soul."

"You are a good man. I cannot be angry."

"Jesus wants to make you His."

"Pray with me."

David did. Afterward he saw that there had been a transformation in Mrs. Schroeder's countenance. She was now a true child of God. Eventually their conversation returned to the baby who had been born. "Rosemary needs to find Jesus, too. Will you pray for her?"

A light shone on Mrs. Schroeder's face. "She can live with me. I have room for them, and I would love to have a baby in the house. And if she lives with me, I can pray for her and never quit until she knows Jesus, too."

David was so surprised. "Why that's a wonderful idea. Wait until I tell her and Josie!"

"Yes. You do that. I hope it makes the woman happy. Then you tell Miss Josephine that you wish to marry her. Maybe then I will forgive you for the frog."

"You'll forgive me anyway. But I will consider it."

That evening, David's manner toward Josie had changed. She attributed it to an emotional day. Josie listened attentively as he freely spoke of Mrs. Schroeder's conversion and about the sappy feelings he always felt after delivering a baby. Her heart melted, and when he told her about Mrs. Schroeder's offer, she shared his excitement. "I can't wait to tell Rosemary. It has also been an eventful, emotional day for me as well."

"How is this?"

"The workhouse received a letter from another workhouse. They want me to come and teach them about our program of personal patronesses."

"That's wonderful. What an opportunity for you."

"I never thought about sharing the idea. It's a bit intimidating."

"Just wear your egg whites and new fragrance, and you'll be a hit."

She playfully pushed him away, but David gripped her forearm and leaned close. "You were wonderful today."

"So were you," she breathed.

"I wanted to do this today at the workhouse. I've thought about it several times since." He inched toward her face, his eyes fixed on her mouth.

Josie held her breath. Could he really be going to kiss her again after all these months? When she saw that he truly intended to, she closed her eyes and waited. His kiss was tender and sweet, just as thrilling as it had been the day they had gone ice skating. Her heart raced.

He groaned. "I can't believe I've wasted all this time. I'm so sorry."

"Sorry about the kiss?" she asked, breathless.

"No, Darling. I've pushed my feelings aside for so long. I think I'm falling in love with you," he whispered huskily. He leaned toward her, and she felt drawn forward.

A clattering sound of boots in the hall broke the enchantment. They quickly pulled apart. Josie's face was hot, and David struggled to compose his expression.

Randolph Cline soon appeared around the corner. He stopped abruptly when he saw them.

"Father, come join us." What else could she say? She sensed David's displeasure.

Randolph dropped easily into a chair and studied David.

"Looks like you're feeling well," David said.

"Yes. Your remedy has done wonders; I'll give you that." Josephine cringed at her father's rude behavior. He met her gaze. "I hear you witnessed a baby's arrival today."

"Not exactly, Father. I didn't see it. But David delivered him."

Mrs. Cline stuck her head in the room. "Randolph! Are you bothering the young people?"

"I don't know. Am I bothering you, Dr. Wheeler?"

"Of course not. We were just discussing the baby."

"How delightful. Randolph loves babies." David looked surprised. "He's an excellent father," Mrs. Cline said.

"I know Josephine thinks very highly of

you, Sir."

"And I prize my daughter. I wish only the best for her."

"Father, really," Josie scolded.

"As do I," David replied. Silence loomed in the room.

"Yes. Well, it's getting late, isn't it," Randolph urged.

David stood and beseeched Josie with his gaze. "I'll be going. It has been a pleasure."

After Josephine shot her father an angry look, she followed David out of the room. Behind them they could hear Mrs. Cline reprimanding her husband for his behavior.

"I'm sorry. He'll come around," Josie said. "Please do not give up on us."

At the door, David smiled. "I'm a patient man." He caressed her cheek. "What I said earlier about my feelings toward you, think about it."

"I'll think of nothing else."

"Keep praying for your father's heart to soften toward me."

Josie nodded, and her heart leapt in anticipation of what lay ahead.

CHAPTER 23

March brought happy days for Josie. Days of falling deeper and deeper in love with David. April was more of the same until one day toward the end of the month when after drawing in a deep breath of air filled with the fragrance of spring flowers, Josephine livened her step. She sensed that any day now David was going to ask her to be his wife. Father's stubborn attitude was the only thing standing in their way. They had discussed that very thing the previous evening when David had left the hat she was on her way now to return.

She opened the clinic's door. The bell jingled, and she stepped inside. The stringent smells of medicine and ointments accosted her. No patients were visible, but she could hear David speaking with someone behind one of the curtained off sections of the room. Tom's head was bent over the desk. He looked up at her.

"Hello, Miss Cline."

"Why so glum, Tom?"

His heavy expression lifted, and she saw a glimmer of yearning, as if he wished to share his burden with her but then thought better of it. "Nothing for you to worry over."

She had grown fond of Tom, especially so in these last two months when she and David had been together so often. "Oh?" She glanced at the curtain again. "I have the time."

The round shoulders sagged, and Josie's heart melted, wondering what could possibly be wrong.

"My time with David is almost finished."

"Is that why you look so sad?"

"I'm glad I'll be able to start my own practice. It's what I've always dreamed of. But my future is being mapped out, and I don't like where it's taking me."

"Who's mapping it out?"

"Dr. Drake and David. They both insist that I either take over the clinic or work at the hospital. But I always dreamed of being a country doctor."

"I see." Josie felt a spark of anger. Dr. Drake was not only managing David's life — overworking him and dragging him away from the clinic and work that he loved — but had managed to control this poor fellow's life as well. And how could David treat Tom the very way he did not like to be treated? "Once you are finished here, will you have met all the requirements to start your own practice?"

"Yes, but I'll need recommendations."

"I believe you need to have courage and tell the doctors that you have your own ideas and that you expect a good recommendation for all your good work."

David's unexpected voice startled her. "Josie, are you trying to steal my right hand away?"

"I'm only suggesting that he do what he wants with his life regardless of what others try to force him to do."

"Force him? I see you do not understand anything about my plans for the clinic."

"Come now, David. No need to get angry. You've said yourself that sometimes Dr. Drake forces his opinions on you."

"Have I? I don't recall saying that."

"Well, it's what I think, that's all."

"And what credentials do you possess that you may give superior counsel over that which Dr. Drake and I have given Tom on this matter?"

Josie felt her mouth drop open at the insult. She stared at David. His face was tight and pale. His eyes flashed with anger.

She felt hurt that he would take sides against her. She glared back at him. "I have the mantle of experience."

"Hah!" he exploded, placing his hands upon his hips and narrowing his eyes.

"Once I worshiped my father as you do the good Dr. Drake. But then I realized that no human is infallible and I do better to listen to my own instincts, allowing for the guidance of my Lord. It is a lesson you have yet to learn." She gave his hat a toss, and it sailed across the room while she strode toward the door. Even in her fury, a part of her hoped that he would call out her name. Tell her to stop. Apologize.

He didn't.

She walked away without looking back. Before she had reached home, her head throbbed. After all these months, she had thought that they had gotten beyond this. The same problem that had plagued their relationship from the very start still reared its ugly head. Although she had grown and become more independent, there would be no relationship with David until he did the same and broke away from his dependence upon Dr. Drake.

Friendships were good. Loyalty and dedication toward those in authority were expected. But if David continued to remain subservient to Drake, then he wasn't the man she wanted to spend her life with.

Her hopes of marriage flashed to her mind. She placed her hand against her mouth to stifle the sobs that started to come forth. Her dreams were tumbling down. David was furious with her. This time she would not be the one to apologize.

Instantly the small voice she was accustomed to listening to asked, *Is your attitude pure?*

She knew it wasn't. She was angry and jealous. She swiped away her tears and tried to get control of her emotions before she passed through the interior of the house. If she could slip unnoticed to her room, maybe she and God could figure things out. Perhaps she needed to get away, take that trip she had been planning and give herself time to cool down and pray.

David watched her go, feeling vindicated for his anger yet knowing he was in the wrong. He did not wish to push her out of his life, and even though he had been striving and planning toward it, if he was honest with himself, he did not even want Tom to take over his clinic. What she said had the ring of truth, and it was humbling. Still, she had no right to interfere in his career —

and just when he had been ready to ask for her hand in marriage. But could he live with such a controlling wife? He had been so shocked at her betraying attitude that he had wanted to force her to back down from her opinion. But she hadn't. And he had pushed her right out the door, maybe right out of his life. David excused himself, walked past a pale Tom, and went home.

What he'd said about her credentials was on target. But her retort was also accurate. In fact, it was what his conscience had been telling him all along. So why had he objected so vehemently? He squeezed his eyes closed. Because he had been putting off his decision about Drake's offer to be his personal assistant. He'd transferred all his problems onto this one issue and tossed it onto her as if everything were her fault.

It was time he made the decision about becoming Drake's assistant. It was his choice. He would deal with that before he dealt with Josephine. If they were to have a life together, he needed to have in his mind what exactly he was offering her. Anyway, if he knew Josephine, she needed time to cool off.

The next day he had barely entered the clinic before his assistant confronted him. "She was right."

David stopped in surprise and turned toward Tom. "I beg your pardon?"

"Miss Cline. What she said. She was right."

"Actually I did not really hear that much of your conversation."

"She saw that I was depressed and asked me why."

"You're depressed? Why didn't you tell me?"

"Men don't talk about such things."

"Ah, but the lovely lady makes a good listener. Women are emotional, caring creatures. Men are logical. You needed her sympathy, not her advice."

"I needed her advice. You need her, too."

"What are you saying?"

"It's always been my dream to be a country doctor. I have no big ambitions. I do not want to work in a hospital. I do not want to do things the way you and Dr. Drake do things. But I do want a good recommendation. I was afraid you wouldn't give me one. She helped me to see that I deserve one."

"Of course you do. I would never hold you back from accomplishing your dream. I'm appalled that you harbored such an idea. And you've done excellent in your training."

"Miss Cline gave me the courage I needed.

I can understand how this all caught you off guard, but while I'm already stretching out my neck, I'm going to add one more thing. If you let her go, you are going to regret it for the rest of your life."

David ran his hands through his hair and stared at the door. His hesitation did not last long. He approached Tom and gripped his shoulder. "Thank you." Then he hastened toward the door, pausing momentarily. "Take over things here, will you?"

"Of course," Tom said with a smile.

"And don't worry about Drake. I'll take care of him for you," David said, and added silently, *And I'm not going to let Drake run my life anymore either. I'm quitting at the hospital, regardless of what he says, and I'm staying at the clinic. If he thinks I'm stagnating, so be it.* It wasn't Drake's fault. They just weren't made out of the same stuff.

"You've never called him that before."

David frowned, trying to understand what Tom meant.

"You left off his title."

David shrugged. "Guess it went with the shackles." He grinned wide. "Josephine's doings."

He stepped outside and hurried across town. If anyone had dared to step in his pathway, he would have mowed them over.

Surprisingly when he confronted Drake, his mentor took his announcement with grace and wished him the best. Savoring the euphoria over the successful outcome of his problem with Drake, he marched toward the Clines'. It was time he pleaded for Josie's forgiveness and begged her to be his wife.

At the door, he was admitted by a servant.

"I'm here to see Miss Cline. I know she won't wish to see me. We've had a spat. Please tell her that she was right. I was wrong, and I've come to apologize."

The servant's face lit, then changed into a broad smile. "I'm sure Miss Cline would be glad to hear that if she were here. But she's not."

CHAPTER 24

"Where is Miss Josephine?" David asked the Clines' servant.

"On a trip. She booked passage on the *Moselle* this morning. I do not know how long she shall be gone. Mrs. Cline has gone to see her off."

"Thank you."

David hurried away. Josephine had been planning a trip to present her ideas about the workhouse, but this reeked of running away. And it frightened him like nothing else ever had. He could not let her go without telling her that he was sorry — that he loved her and wanted to marry her.

His steps hastened to a run. He heard the *Moselle*'s whistle and instinctively knew that he was too late. Still, he couldn't stop running. If need be, he would yell it out loud enough for all those gathered on the docks to hear that he loved her. At least she would go away knowing he wasn't the stubborn fool that he appeared to be.

As he rounded the next corner, he saw the great ship pulling out of the dock. He groaned. She had promised she wouldn't take the *Moselle* but a slower, safer ship. Josie was not to be seen. Nor Mrs. Cline. He paused on the edge of the small crowd to catch his breath. A man nearby who leaned on an ivory cane acknowledged him.

"Do you know the *Moselle's* next stop?"

"Fulton. She's a beauty. The swiftest vessel . . ."

David nodded and turned to go. He didn't have time to converse.

"Doctor?"

"Mrs. Cline! I'm so glad to see you. Where's Josie?"

Her voice was stilted. She sniffed. "Josephine just left for St. Louis. I don't suppose you had anything to do with this." Her red eyes accused.

"I'm afraid I did. That's why I need to speak with her. I must go."

"But, Doctor . . ."

Without even answering, David started to jog. It was only a mile up the river to Fulton, Josie's next stop, but he needed to zigzag through the city to reach it.

An inexplicable force propelled him forward. He lost sight of the ship and knew that everything depended upon how long she would remain docked. He could only hope that he would make it in time.

He rounded the corner and saw the *Moselle* was still there. Nearly out of breath he strained to continue, but then his heart sank. She started to leave the harbor. Still, he could not give up. He pressed forward with all his might. He could see passengers crowded together on the upper deck. The people who had gathered on the shore were cheering the *Moselle* off. It looked as if she were going to participate in a race with another ship. The noise was too loud. Josie would never hear him, even if he could find her.

And then it happened. While he was still a great distance away, his chest burning from the unaccustomed exertion, the most horrible tragedy he could ever witness took place.

A deafening explosion, as if a mine of gunpowder had gone off, blew the *Moselle* apart before his very eyes. The deck of passengers was blown into the air to instant destruction. He jerked to a stop, unable to understand the magnitude of the situation and at the same time knowing he didn't want to believe what he was seeing. The sounds of the explosion and steam and destruction came first, then the screams of those witnessing the event. His own scream joined theirs as he bent over in grief and screamed "No! No! No!" again and again.

As if in a dream, he raised his head and looked toward the scene. He must find Josie. He ran to the edge of the crowd and began to push through, adding his voice to all those around him who were searching for loved ones. "Josephine. Josie. Josie."

Someone pulled on his coat and would not release him. "Help us, Doctor. Please."

As much as he wanted to hope that Josie was alive and that he would find her, he could not neglect the wounded who needed his medical attention. Working through a veil of tears in an environment that seemed surreal, and many times with trembling hands, he went from patient to patient doing what he could to revive nearly drowned individuals. He set bones, applied tourniquets, doing whatever he could without any supplies. But as he worked, he bitterly accused himself. It was all his fault. If he hadn't gotten angry, Josie never would have been on that ship. All his fault and what was he going to do without her?

Soon all of Cincinnati's citizens learned of the news. Other physicians arrived on the scene, and even those without medical training, to do what they could to help the injured, console those who lost loved ones, and to search for missing persons. His assistant found him, and once David had his medical bag, he began to treat those who had scalded skin. Yet his ears and eyes were on the alert. Where was his dear Josie? Could he bear it if he found her?

"Doctor!" David looked up. It was Randolph Cline. His face was twisted with grief. "Have you seen my Josie?"

"No. I'm just about done here. Can you help hold this? Then I'll join you to search for her."

The man assisted, but it was as if he were in a daze. Afterward, David went with him and together they started to work their way through the confusion.

It seemed forever and at the same time as if they had not gone far at all until Otis Washburn saw them. "Doctor. Can you help here?"

The reporter's woman friend had splinters in her arms. David took an instrument from his bag and began to remove them, allowing Randolph to help. As they worked, the reporter confessed his regrets.

"We were on the shore watching. It's all my fault she's hurt." The reporter started to weep unashamedly.

"Nonsense." David identified with the man, wanting to take all the blame for everything upon his own shoulders. He gripped the other's arm. "It was an accident."

"No. The newspapers' praise of the speed and power of the *Moselle* no doubt goaded the captain and owners to race against others, taking chances with the boilers. I never dreamed something like this would occur."

"Your friend is going to be fine."

"Father? David!"

At the sound of her voice, David spun round, searching the crowd for his beloved. She was alive and running toward them. She hurled herself into her father's arms. They wept and clung to each other in desperation. After a time, Randolph eased her away. "I thought I had lost you. So many things went through my mind. Your doctor has been courageous." She looked at her father, as if to ask for permission, and he nodded.

David gave Randolph a grateful look and drew Josephine close, whispering against her temple. "I came for you, but you'd already gone. How did you manage to escape harm?"

"I saw you at the port when we left, speaking to Mother. I knew I could not run away from you so I got off at Fulton. I started hurrying to find you. But when the ship exploded, I must have fainted. When I came to, I was confused."

"I know that it is selfish and weak of me to rejoice that you are alive in the midst of this tragedy. But I cannot help it. I . . ."

Josie pulled away. "I know." Her face paled. "I'm going to be sick."

David assisted her and held her until she was feeling stronger. She swiped her tears away. "You saved my life, showing up that way."

Randolph Cline, who had been listening to their private conversation and hovering ready to help his daughter, repeated, "You saved her life. How can I ever repay you?"

David shook his head. "It was my fault she was on that ship. I almost got her killed. I'll understand if you never want to see me again."

Randolph frowned. "It was an accident. Isn't that what you told Otis Washburn?"

Meanwhile Josie gazed helplessly about her. "We must do something to help these people."

Otis Washburn gave David a wave. He and his woman friend leaned upon each other for support. All around them were huddles of people embracing, giving aid.

"There's still much to do," David said.

"I'll help, too," Randolph offered.

CHAPTER 25

David and Tom worked through the night at the clinic. The door opened and David looked up with surprise. "Mr. Cline."

"May we talk?"

David glanced around the clinic. "It's full in here. Do you want to step outside?" He nodded. It seemed inappropriate to hear the birds singing at the top of their lungs after such devastation the day before. "How can I help you?"

Cline cleared his throat. "I wish to apologize for the way I've thwarted your work."

"Accepted."

"That's all?"

"I hold nothing against you, Sir. How could I? I love your daughter."

"Let me explain. When I met my wife, she was enamored of Drake. I thought I'd lose her to him. For years I had to listen to his praises from her. It had nothing to do with you."

"Drake was a happily married man. And Mrs. Cline seems very happy with you."

"I know. I've been a fool."

"Well, if it's any consolation, I've learned to let go of him also. To do a bit more thinking on my own, with the Lord's help."

"Sound advice for someone so young. Quite humbling, Doctor."

"Not at all. It's the advice your daughter gave me. She's the wise one."

Randolph beamed. "She's something, isn't she?"

David cleared his throat. "Perhaps this is the right time to ask you about her. For her hand, I mean. I know I'm not what you intended for her, but I promise to take care of her and cherish her."

Randolph Cline exhaled deeply. "I suspected this was coming."

"If it helps, be assured that even though I don't have much to offer her, I believe we're like-minded."

Randolph burst into boisterous laughter. "That's a good one. No man is like-minded with any woman. But you'll do good to listen to her. I'll give you my approval, but of course it's Josie who will have to make up her own mind. And money isn't a problem. She has her own inheritance. And I don't believe I'll have to worry about you squandering it." His eyes narrowed. "But don't be giving it all away either. I'll have to give you some lessons in business management. I believe we may make a good team." He extended his hand. "Thanks for saving my Josie."

David pumped the older man's hand. "Thank you, Sir. You won't regret it. I promise."

When Randolph departed, David felt like joining the birds in their song.

"What is it that you have to show me?" Josie asked, her expression wary. Although the weeks since the explosion had been hard for everyone in Cincinnati with the loss of loved ones, friends, and neighbors, she had been delirious with contentment now that her father and David had made peace. But today everyone had been acting peculiar — as if they were in on a secret.

Her mother's eyes had twinkled. She and her father seemed closer than ever. Josie knew that the explosion had affected many families that way. Everyone was thankful for their loved ones.

"You'll see. Close your eyes and take my hand," David urged.

She did as he suggested and allowed him to lead her from the waiting room of his clinic into one of the curtained off areas.

"You can open them now."

She did, and instantly they brimmed with tears. Looking up at him with all the love she felt, she said, "You can be so romantic."

"I know I can get in a rut. Please forgive me."

"I do."

Mrs. Schroeder peeked her head inside the curtain and winked at her.

"Please, sit down. Enjoy." David motioned Josie to a chair. She took in the table, cloth, flowers, and the dinner that Mrs. Schroeder had prepared and intended to chaperone. He seated himself across from her.

"A sleigh ride would have suited the occasion better, but I am not a magician," he said.

She clasped both of his outstretched hands across the table. "I believe with the Lord's help you can accomplish most anything."

"Your encouragement, your very presence is the one thing that has been missing in my life."

"I have not been encouraging to you?"

"That is not what I meant. But I am not to be rushed. We must take our time here and enjoy this moment."

She gazed into his emotion-filled eyes and

saw the love that he held for her. "So what is the occasion?"

"The celebration of our love. I love you, Josie."

"I love you, too." She caressed his cheek. "You are a good man."

"Marry me."

She caught her breath but did not hesitate for an instant. She had waited too long for him to ask. "Yes!"

He chuckled at her eagerness and leaned across the table, and she could see that he was intent upon kissing her. She leaned forward also, but they were still lacking several inches from being able to meet. He smiled. "I see I need practice at this. Come here, *speziell Dame*."

"*Stattlich Doktor.*" She giggled nervously.

Still holding her hand, he rose and drew her up and toward him. She slid into his arms and returned his kiss. When they drew apart, he pressed his face into her hair. "Oh, Josie. You're wearing lavender again."

She slowly drew away. "I love you so." Then she smiled. "Can we go tell Mother and Father?"

"After our dinner."

"Oops." She clamped a hand across her mouth. "I forgot."

"Let's eat, then we'll go tell your parents.

258

And maybe after that we'll visit Tom. He's getting ready to leave soon. I'm glad we can give him the news before he moves on."

"Yes. And you'll want to tell Dr. Drake."

"He stopped in today. It was the first I'd seen him since I'd resigned from the hospital and turned down his offer of being his personal assistant. He wanted to make sure there were no hard feelings. He really is an amazing man. But he's gone now on another trip. I am eager to write about our engagement to my family."

"I hope they can all come to the wedding." They stared intently into each other's eyes. She thought about how much they had learned, how far they had come to get to this point of love and trust.

"Your father and I are agreed upon one thing."

"Oh? What is that?" she asked.

"We don't want you taking that trip to St. Louis alone."

"So now it's you *and* Father conniving together and telling me what to do."

"A nice switch, isn't it?"

"Yes. So are you going to come with me when I take the trip? Is that what you are so tactfully trying to say?"

"Maybe. We could combine it with a honeymoon."

"I believe the three of us finally agree. And I believe this calls for another kiss, Dr. Spokes."

But before they could seal their vows, the curtain moved. Mrs. Schroeder, who wore a smile of approval, quickly jerked it closed again.

ABOUT THE AUTHOR

Dianne Christner and her husband make their home in Scottsdale, Arizona, enjoying the beauty of the desert. However, it is fond memories of her childhood spent in Ohio that inspired this book. After years of working as an executive secretary, she is happy to be able to spend her time at home writing or traveling and researching. If you enjoyed this book, she invites you to visit her website www.diannechristner.com so that you can meet her and her family members and follow her latest writing endeavors.

The employees of Thorndike Press hope you have enjoyed this Large Print book. All our Thorndike and Wheeler Large Print titles are designed for easy reading, and all our books are made to last. Other Thorndike Press Large Print books are available at your library, through selected bookstores, or directly from us.

For information about titles, please call:
(800) 223-1244

or visit our Web site at:
www.gale.com/thorndike
www.gale.com/wheeler

To share your comments, please write:
Publisher
Thorndike Press
295 Kennedy Memorial Drive
Waterville, ME 04901